CROSSING TO FREEDOM

CROSSING TO FREEDOM

Virginia Frances Schwartz

Cover by Greg Ruhl

Scholastic Canada Ltd.
Toronto New York London Auckland Sydney
Mexico City New Delhi Hong Kong Buenos Aires

Scholastic Canada Ltd.
604 King Street West, Toronto, Ontario M5V 1E1, Canada

Scholastic Inc.
557 Broadway, New York, NY 10012, USA

Scholastic Australia Pty Limited
PO Box 579, Gosford, NSW 2250, Australia

Scholastic New Zealand Limited
Private Bag 94407, Botany, Manukau 2163, New Zealand

Scholastic Children's Books
Euston House, 24 Eversholt Street, London NW1 1DB, UK

Library and Archives Canada Cataloguing in Publication

Schwartz, Virginia Frances
Crossing to freedom / Virginia Frances Schwartz.

ISBN 978-0-545-98978-7

1. Fugitive slaves--Canada--Juvenile fiction. 2. Black
Canadians--Ontario--History--Juvenile fiction. I. Title.

PS8587.C5786C76 2010   jC813'.6   C2010-901690-4

6 5 4 3 2 1   Printed in Canada   116   10 11 12 13 14

*For those who crossed over
from slavery to freedom
and all those left behind*

CONTENTS

*"When we land on Canaan's shore,
we'll meet forever more."*

— from "O Brothers, Don't Get Weary"

PREFACE

Back then, all those years ago, I didn't own words the way I do now. Didn't guess their power. How they can carry your wishes across years and miles and wrap around someone far from reach. It was Mister Dillon who first drilled letters into my mind so my hand would know what to do.

But it was Old Ezekiel, the one who remembered, who set me to wondering.

"If no one tells the story," he said, "then it's not real, what happened. No one will know about these scars inside you or anythin' about your grandpa if you don't say it."

And now these words come to me shining like silver nickels in the dark. Whole spillings of them to sprinkle over these pages.

Here are the names of the free, I say, and how they came to be that way.

Chapter 1
THUNDER WATER

June 1857

HERE'S WHAT I REMEMBER of that night.

Up 'til then, we had a plan. Up 'til then, we were headed straight to freedom.

We were riding close to the border crossing between New York and Canada West. The three of us were tucked in the back of the wagon, buried beneath a shipment of woolly horse blankets. So damp and cool, our clothes felt wet. Nearby was a roar of water rushing, louder and louder, like guns exploding. Nobody seemed to hear it but me. I was the only one awake in the back.

"Stay way down under, should we stop," one of the drivers had warned us.

Four silver dollars Grandpa Jacob paid them to drive us across the last leg north to a place called Buffalo. No telling how many eyes watching in such a border town, they warned us. Couldn't walk in plain sight there. Slavecatchers. Customs agents. Smugglers. White folks who'd turn you in because the colour of your skin up north brought good reward money. So we spent the last of our savings and took the ride.

Beside me, Levi slept deep, hot as a coal oven. Other slaves warned us about taking the underground road with Levi. Said he came from trouble and was headed that way again. I knew there'd been something between him and Master Tiller, but Grandpa swore Levi was the only man he knew crazy enough to guide us to freedom.

3

"Who'd want to bring a string bean like me — an old man of fifty — and a pea pod of an eleven-year-old boy with him across the country?" Grandpa laughed. "Nobody!"

The first I heard of these plans was the March night Grandpa woke me to run.

"Solomon, we got to leave the plantation right now. Think my legs gonna hold up if we wait one more year? Can't wait for freedom to come to us. Gotta go where it is. You are strong enough to run on the underground."

Seemed to me I was scrawny, bone with flesh stretched over it. Tupelo honey brown. My ears flapping too big for my face. Not like Levi. You never saw a bigger man. Built like a tree, Master Tiller bragged. My two hands couldn't fit around his upper arm. Levi threw his head back and laughed whenever I tried to do it. Seemed he lived high up in the treetops. And now he was right here beside me, sleeping.

Grandpa and Levi drifted in and out. They'd been awake for days, always on guard. But I had slept through the two long days since we jumped on the wagon. All those miles were behind us now, about eight hundred from our Georgia plantation, Levi figured. So few miles left to go. When the wagon stopped for supplies earlier that day, and the drivers hopped off, nobody stirred. But my eyes flew open. I waited and waited for those drivers. Seemed they took too long. They didn't throw any food in the back either, like they promised, when they returned. The wagon drove on into darkness. One turn in the road. Then another.

That's when the noise began, a forever whir that pounded louder and louder like we were headed straight into danger. I sat up to listen. One of the drivers' voices drifted. " . . . hundred . . . gonna be rich . . ."

There was some arguing back and forth between them. The wind of rushing waters whipped away most of what they said.

But I kept on listening. That's when I heard them say the name, then, ". . . tie that Levi down . . . Get the pistol read— "

I sat up lightning-rod straight. In the next second I shook Grandpa awake. He came to slow. Soon as I touched Levi, he jerked, his eyes burning.

"You seen a ghost, boy?" Levi asked.

The words got stuck somewhere between my stomach and my throat. That's how it'd always been. There were things in my heart I never learned to speak aloud. Even thinking the truth or meeting the overseer's eye could earn me a whipburn. So I made myself numb, no thoughts at all. Looking like I didn't know anything. Then I was safe.

Grandpa turned my head toward his, trying to read my eyes. His long fingers held me still. "What's gone wrong, Solomon?"

I could never fool Grandpa. He knew me through and through without my ever saying much. Both men leaned in close so I could whisper what I overheard.

Levi's breath seemed to pass out of his body, leaving his chest flat. "Master put out the word about me far and wide. Never gonna forget what I did."

He crawled out of the blankets toward the back of the wagon.

"Don't go without us!" Grandpa's voice rose up.

"You crazy, old man? If these men know about me so quick, then others know about me too. Must be posters everywhere givin' some reason for turning me in. If you are found with me, they're gonna drag you back too. You're not strong enough to take the beatin' we'll get. Go on alone. Be safer for you."

Levi opened the back flaps. Came a sound like a roar. It built up, minute by minute, whisking our words away. Sounded like wind rushing wild.

"Must be near the Falls. Such a dangerous place!" he said. "Can't cross there. We come the wrong way. They led us too far above Buffalo."

"Then we're sure not headed for the ferry crossin' like we asked," Grandpa said. "We are all in trouble. You can't bail out without us, Levi. We three come this far. We'll go on together."

Grandpa crawled right up there beside him. Levi's eyes lit like embers and around his mouth, such twitching. Grandpa Jacob breathed deep and slow and set his hand on Levi's arm. Minutes passed. All the while, my ears were like open doors listening for the drivers' voices over the thump of the wheels.

"For the boy." Grandpa looked straight at him.

Levi sighed, opened the flap wide and turned to me. "Be light as a feather now."

I hit the ground like a rabbit kicking its hind legs. Levi leaped down like a cougar running soundless from the first step. But Grandpa fell to the ground and rolled. It took some minutes for him to right himself.

We lit out for the woods at the side of the road. Such a scattering of feet and pumping of heartbeats. I prayed nobody heard either one. The thunder of the waters was so loud, you could have yelled and it'd sound like a whisper. Down the slope, we slid closer and closer to those roaring waters below. If the drivers ran after us, there was nowhere to go but straight into them. And neither Grandpa or I could swim.

Chapter 2
BORDERLAND

THICK AND DARK IT WAS AS WE HEADED through the woods, down to the Niagara River. Trees rushing past, heads ducking, rocks tripping Grandpa up. Snapping of dried branches as we tore through. We took no caution to be quiet. Didn't follow the usual rules Levi set. This time we just ran. I'd learned to be quick on my heels like a rabbit bolting at the bang of a shotgun. One minute you see him, next second he's gone. We were running loose and wild like the water below.

That river made me dizzy. It looked a mile across to the other side. Wherever I turned, there was water. From streams and pathways on all sides, water led downhill into this river. In such a hurry to get to the Falls, I suppose, and be free. Rushing every which way, backwards and sideways, twisting like snakes. Running downhill, angry at anything that got in its path. So strong, it'd knock a tree flat if it met up with one. Seemed greedy to me.

I snuck a look back before we jumped downhill, though they told me not to. The sound of wagon wheels creaked over the bumpy path. I prayed the drivers hadn't felt the weight of us leave, we did it so light. Or maybe the swirling waters were rushing too loud. How long we had before they discovered us gone, no way of guessing.

Many lights shone in the distance above the road. Looked like a town way beyond. But we followed Levi's lead upstream, far beneath the road. We'd been running together most every night since late winter. Even with my eyes closed, I could see Levi. He was in my head. His back looks like a letter, a slave who could read told me. Like a *V*, whatever that is. So wide at his shoulders, you could set a water bucket on each one and they'd stay right there. Narrow at his waist. Not a pinch of fat. Mostly you had the feeling when Levi was around that he was the strong among us.

But even though we were with him, we had never been loose in a border town next to such a wild river, a river meant for crossing only in a boat, over ground so slippery wet my feet didn't hold to it, but slid down the sloped land.

Through the trees, Grandpa's breath blew raspy like he couldn't grab enough air. Maybe it was the speed we set, but he seemed out of breath too soon, one leg trailing behind. Before, it was me who was always the last one.

Keep up . . . I turned my head, saying the words silently, from inside.

Grandpa nodded, struggling to slip around one boulder after another. We hiked hard and fast, and my legs got that trembling again, not setting down firm, cramping some. Half the night must have passed and we ran silent, drumming down on the ground. Seemed we had no bodies at all except for our legs.

Sometimes the thoughts came as they always do. Passing through me from one side and leaving out the other side like wind. *Are the drivers turnin' around now? Are they searchin' for our tracks in the mud?*

Levi saved me from such thinking. He lifted his wide hand flat in the air. Sign to stop. We stood still as trees. Chests heaving wild at first, then slowly easing down. Couldn't feel our own heartbeats anymore though they'd been banging in our ears all the while. The world popped back. Rustling of leaves. Dank smell of moss. Water racing.

Levi turned his head like an owl, studying each tree, every gust of wind, smelling and feeling things in the night that I don't even want to think about. After long minutes, he walked over to us.

"By now, the drivers will find the wagon empty and turn around, thinkin' to trap us by that ferry. So we got to change our plans. We'll hide here for the night. No houses above us."

"But we're headed the same way as them," Grandpa said.

"They have to stick to the road. Can't follow us through these woods. Besides, we got to trust this river. It's our only chance. Kind of wild right now, headin' downhill, but farther up, got to be easier. Suppose that's why the ferry crosses there."

"How we gonna get across? The boy and I don't swim. Never seen water this fearsome."

Levi shrugged. "If we don't cross one way or another, we're gonna get caught. This is the borderland. We're real close to Canada now. Slavecatchers roam like hunters."

The sky gave us a signal. A lifting of the dark. First light coming, it warned.

"Let's settle in," Grandpa decided. "We'll move ahead at night, like always, and figure it out."

Levi sunk down and raked old leaves in piles and we joined him. Soon we had enough to cover us, pressing the leaves on top of us like graves.

"Here, Solomon, there's some left." Grandpa dug into his pocket.

He handed me hard chunks of cornmeal for cooking. But

we couldn't light a fire. So you stored those chunks on one side of your cheeks like a squirrel and let your spit work on it. Sometime later, you could swallow because it'd be softer.

"Likely to give us all a stomach ache." Grandpa grinned. "But that's better than hunger. Rest now, Solomon. Not a word 'til deep dark."

Beneath me, the cool ground felt hard. Yesterday, resting flat in that wagon, the other side was still laid out golden in my mind, full of cornfields, roasted venison, berry pies, and maybe even news of my gone-away father. All the stories Grandpa had been filling my ear full about Canada, ever since we ran. All those nights on the underground road when we hid, hungry and cold, as I fell asleep to Grandpa's whispered promises of the new land.

We had almost touched it.

But freedom slipped away that night. Now we had another journey ahead. Nowhere was safe. Though we had outwitted hounds and slavecatchers for four months, here was something we hadn't figured on.

All that day, as we lay still, barely breathing, the river never stopped talking. Seemed like it was scolding us. Daring us to try and cross. *The way is blocked*, I thought I heard it say. *You can't cross over here.* It felt like we were still back home, listening to old Master Tiller say we were nothing and going nowhere but to the fields.

Chapter 3
GHOST WALKERS

RUNNING ALL NIGHT AND WAKING IN THE WOODS someplace you don't know where, was something you'd think you'd get used to after four months. Don't ever get used to it. The whir of wagon wheels, drivers yelling and voices on the wind woke us early.

Inside our leaf graves, we froze. Our listening went out far beyond our bodies, into the half-light, trying to guess what we could not see. Above us, the ground shook. Voices shouted, then trailed away. We must have stopped close to a road, with such comings and goings. But no wagon stopped. Everyone seemed to be hurrying straight to the place we were headed.

I breathed shallow and did not move. Beside me, Grandpa did not stir either, though I knew he was awake. He'd be worried about me most likely, wishing he had a hickory nut to slip into my hand. He always saved something in his pocket to surprise me with. Usually a peanut or a dried berry. Once a marble he found. Or a slingshot he had carved back home. But his pockets were empty now.

All that day, I did not sleep. Instead, I thought about how I got here, lying near a road in the borderland. Grandpa was all I got. My ma was sixteen when she birthed me and seventeen when she was sold away. I don't recall her face at all. They say my pa, Grandpa's son, took the underground road when I was six. He didn't tell us before he went. Just one morning, there

11

was an empty spot beside me and I awoke to Master kicking up a storm. Tried not to think of my pa anymore. Be just a never-going-away pain if I did. Grandpa Jacob was the only one who'd been with me my whole life; he was father and mother both.

Finally, when I was settling into deep sleep, some deer leaped, their hooves setting down in one firm point nearby. Got to be dusk. *Wait a little longer,* I reminded myself, *to be sure the dark drops down to hide us.* But the time from dusk to dark seemed forever that evening. I stared through the leaves until all I could see was black.

Levi sat up first, long after the last of the wagons rumbled by. He listened long. He didn't even shake any leaves off, just stood up and started walking fast. So we followed, me on rabbit feet, Grandpa taking up the rear, slow and steady. It was a dark night, full of clouds with spits of rain. But the river gave off a kind of glow and if we got near it, we could see some. But mostly we walked in the dark like ghosts, not knowing where we were going. Moving our feet ahead like something was pulling us. Rushing like something was chasing us.

Ghost walkers, we were. Invisible. Haunted.

What would happen if the drivers found us and sent us back? I'd seen poor Job yanked back by slavecatchers, then strung upside down from a tree, from sun-up to sunset three long days one scorching July. When they let him down, they cut deep into the flesh behind his ankles so he'd never run again. And old Enos, Levi's pa, who ran away more than once, forever shuffling across the plantation with both ankles chained together, setting all the hounds to barking.

Let them not find us, I thought. *Even if I never eat until we get to Canada.*

Sometimes an empty belly is a good thing, I remembered Levi saying a while back. When your belly's empty, it keeps you running. You keep hoping to run into something — a safe place, a barn warmed by animal breath, leftover food. And it makes your mind clear as a star in a blue-black sky.

But what if you had too many nights of an empty belly and your legs shake with every step, you don't know whether it's hunger or fear or growing pains? I never asked Levi that. I took to arguing in my head with him. Back and forth, I questioned him. Rammed my complainings straight at him. Such things I would never say aloud. Not one word had I dared say to anyone in charge. The Master, the overseer, even the men who patrolled our cabins, never heard my voice. Could never tell what Levi would do if I spoke up. Either laugh until his guts split, or ignore me. I learned never to speak my mind.

The stars lit up, a few at first. Then the whole sky cleared. Hour after hour, more stars dotted the sky. Then, just like that, it happened. A *click*, then a *clang* of something metal, leaves flying around me. When I turned, Grandpa was twisted in mid-air like he was flying. He fell to the ground, kicking up a storm.

We rushed over. A wide metal trap clamped down on his right ankle. It was pegged to the ground. Grandpa couldn't take one step farther.

Levi grabbed two big stones and set one on each side of the trap. "Hold on Jacob, while I get you loose."

I reached for Grandpa's hand and squeezed. Up close, his face looked sunken around the mouth and his black and white speckled hair pointed every which way.

The trap was so old and rusty, it wouldn't budge. It grabbed deep into the bare flesh of Grandpa's ankle like a jaw of huge teeth. I pressed my lips together to stop myself from screaming.

Terrible creaking and groaning of that trap as Levi pushed and pried. Finally it gave way. When Grandpa's foot came free, Levi bent close to it.

"You can't walk on that ankle. Bone's likely broken. And we can't rest here so close to this trap. Whoever set this, be it for animal or runaway, will be back."

Grandpa was getting ready to speak but Levi gave him no time to argue. He heaved my grandpa up over his shoulder like a fallen log. We walked deeper into the woods. The moon followed us, peeking out in slivers at times, then hiding again. In and out it did this for the rest of the night. Even the stars hid. At last, Levi set Grandpa down by the river. His foot dangled sideways, twisting from his leg unnatural. Levi set Grandpa's foot deep into the cold river.

"That eases it up some. But what hurts most — " Grandpa pointed to the top of his leg " — is here, where I fell out of that wagon. It aches deep."

Levi tried to touch the side of his hip but Grandpa opened his mouth so wide, I thought he would scream. His breath came panting hard; his lips turned down, bitter. He and Levi looked at one another. So dark their eyes.

We both had to hold Grandpa up as we searched for a place to rest, one of us on each side. The weight of him was heavy though he was a slip of a man. Where the trees grew thickest, we set him down. Levi set Grandpa's foot high on top a rock, then disappeared to see what was around us. I dragged leaves and evergreen branches for our blankets. Then I gathered the whirling seed wings fallen on the ground beneath the maples. They were dry and hard that June, but I pretended they were peanuts. Grandpa and I crunched away and waited on Levi.

Suddenly Grandpa bit his lips and squeezed his eyes shut.

His breath got short again. He and I were alone and he was hurting. Nothing I could do but lean over him and watch. Afraid to even whisper in case somebody was nearby. So I did what he did once when I had shooting belly pains after eating too many green apples. Laid my hand on his chest and breathed slow and deep, hoping he'd match my breath.

Soon Grandpa was sleeping. As I built up leaves around him, rustling drifted to my ears. I tunnelled beneath the leaves and held still. Footsteps stopped by my head.

"Fooled me good." Levi laughed. "Almost stepped on your head."

I sat up. Levi's eyes strayed to Grandpa.

"Good he's restin'. That pain sure knocked him out. The road's farther away now. We stopped a short walk from the outskirts of a town. Nobody's out."

"What are we gonna do about Grandpa?" I had to ask.

"Tomorrow you and me will go to town. See if we can get help. Directions. Or food."

With that, I handed him some maple seeds from my pocket. He munched down hard, looking off into the distance. We could see clear all around now. The moon was full and rose up out of the darkness.

"Look at that!" He pointed.

Levi was looking straight at the river. When he crawled toward it, I followed behind, staying low down.

"Just like I figured," he said. "The water is gettin' narrow. Not so twisty. Bet if we followed it upriver, it'd let us cross."

For the first time, I saw the other side. Promised Land, some called it when they whispered about Canada, using the old name from the Bible stories. It's what you wished for when you had nothing to call your own. Though it looked much the same as it did here, with trees and a high bank, it was not the same. Over there, not so far away, about the distance from our old cabins to the fields, was freedom. The water swirled and gurgled, white and calm in the moonlight. It seemed to dance and laugh now. I dipped my hands right into that cold water and swallowed a big handful.

This water has touched the land that has no slaves, I told myself. This water knows freedom.

Chapter 4
SEPARATION

JUST BEFORE DUSK THE NEXT DAY, Levi whistled. Sign to go scouting. I bust loose out of those leaves.

Grandpa poked his head out but did not stir. "Stay safe," he whispered.

He hadn't stirred much all that day. Though I'd heard groaning and even sighing from beneath his piles of leaves, I dared not budge or say a word to him.

"Mark," Levi ordered me.

He meant for me to mark our trail. In case we had to run back fast, it would show us the way. I got a sneaky way of doing it. Pinching leaves of bushes way down low on their underbelly, where tall men wouldn't think of bending down to check. I split the biggest leaf down the middle and placed a stone on a nearby leaf, little signs I'd been there that only I would know.

Past the road, through the pines, slipping between the tall maples, at last we looked out at the town Levi said must be Buffalo. No wide fields. No farms. No distance between things. Here, streets filled with houses jammed side by side like too many teeth. Horses pulling fine carriages. People walking home in the dim lamplight. Lights aglow in windows. If I hadn't seen it with my own eyes, I would never have believed it: white folks and coloured, side by side in the streets. Some in working clothes. Others in wide dresses carting baskets. All strolling at ease in the evening where anyone could see them, even slowing down to look in shop windows.

Levi pointed to one small shop, its window bright. "Lookit there. A coloured man hammerin' away. He's all by himself inside, so maybe he'll help."

We both flew closer in, behind the next set of trees. On the door of the man's shop was a sign with some words and a painting of shoes.

Levi jerked his head toward the street. "Walk beside me. If you stop and stare with big eyes, someone will grab us. Look like you belong and are just about your business."

Levi stepped into the path behind an old white couple. He kept his head down and his cap pulled over the side of his face. I blinked. He disappeared down the street.

My fists tightened. That Levi thinks something and the next second he's doing it. I had no choice but to start my feet walking and try to catch up with him. A white man passed me by like he didn't see me. But an old lady tipped her bonnet a little, so I knew I was there. Finally I was beside Levi. We both crossed the street together in front of the shoe shop.

Outside the shop was a big tree with posters nailed all over it. Black words snaking across them. Didn't know what they said, but I sure knew the face staring out of one: Levi.

Without even a breath's pause, Levi opened the door of the shoemaker's shop. A bell set to ringing. The man looked up in the middle of tapping a shoe. We pressed flat against the far wall inside, panting.

"Drop down," he ordered us. "Crawl to the back room."

He wiped his hands, then walked over to stand by his shop window for long minutes, looking out into the street. Afterwards, he followed us into a tiny room. "Got the look of the woods about you. You runaways?"

Levi nodded.

"Let me see your face," he asked of Levi. "Take off your hat." The man gasped. "I've looked at your picture every day for the last two months. Got a big reward out on you. Seven hundred dollars! That price makes folks real greedy. Not safe for you and the boy to be seen in Buffalo. Better cover your face out there."

Levi looked like a hurt animal. "But *you* are here in plain sight and nobody's botherin' you. That's why we came in."

"I hold free papers. Paid my master for them. Been here six years. Everybody knows me. Anyone tries to catch hold of me and drag me back to Alabama, the judge in this town would never allow it — he's my best customer. But you still belong to somebody and looks like they're payin' plenty to get you back."

Free, he said. Living on the wrong side of the border and working for himself. He wasn't skinny either, or worn-down looking like Grandpa. And he was wearing fancy high leather boots just like Master Tiller, with such a shine to them they caught the light of the lamp and glowed.

"Runaways risk trouble here in Buffalo, so they ride the ferry across and travel up to the settlements inland, far from any border. Sent my own wife and children there. They had no free papers."

"We got more trouble than just my face," Levi said. He told the shopkeeper about Grandpa's accident, the ferry, and his worry about where we could cross now.

"You got a price on your head, so no one must see you. Doesn't make it easy to get around. Go to the Baptist Church over on Michigan Street. They gonna figure somethin' out."

The shopkeeper lifted a basket and took out some bread, apples and dried beef. "All I got," he said. "Make it last."

He gave us directions to the church, some streets away.

Meanwhile, he stepped outside, checked up and down the street, then nodded. We walked out, heads straight up, like we just left our shoes for shining. Never mind that our feet were bare.

"Take the trail back to your grandpa," Levi told me. "I'm headin' to the church."

I tugged on his sleeve. "Let me go with you. Grandpa says we got to stick together, remember?"

Levi's eyes shifted from me to the street. No way of telling what he was thinking with his face mostly hidden in shadow. In the dim lamplight of this big town, he suddenly seemed a stranger.

"I got to figure out a new plan. Be back later. Go straight back to your grandpa."

He jammed some of the bread into his mouth, handed me the rest of the food, then in a few strides slipped halfway down the street. I had to stop myself from running after him. Nowhere to go then but toward the maples. The way back was not long, but it was deep dark with no moon up yet. I bent down close to the dirt to feel the underside of bushes for the signs I left. But it was the sound of the water, the tilt of the land down and down, that led me back.

I came to the pile of leaves by the river. It was still.

"Grandpa?" I whispered.

His head slowly rose up like some turtle sniffing air. I dropped the bread and apple into his open hands and scooted to the river for a handful of water. He drank with his eyes on me, not touching his food until I munched down on mine.

"You leave Levi behind?" he asked.

"A man told him about some church so he went on by himself. Said they might help us."

We sat up in the dark a while, watching the water run toward the Falls. It took our minds over to watch it. It seemed so sure it was going someplace. Talking all the while out loud. So free and wild, nothing could ever stop it.

Every once in a while, Grandpa grunted. His ankle was swollen three times the size it should be, hot to the touch. I scurried back and forth to the river to scoop up handfuls of water to cool it down some. He sighed each time I did that.

"I should be takin' care of you. But you are growin' so fast, you're takin' care of me. Makes me proud, Solomon. Tomorrow, I'll get up. Can't move any now. This hip is actin' up too much."

Grandpa laid back down and I covered him from head to toe with leaves. He was the one who always tucked me in, but he was shivering now though it was not cold. We were so close to freedom, he just had to hold on.

That Levi was a long time coming. My mind kept circling around the beef jerky in my pocket. Been weeks since we ate any meat. If only I could lick it some just to get a taste. But if I did that, the whole piece would be gone. I had to save it for tomorrow.

So I stopped those thoughts and gave my mind something new to chew on instead: the other side. Slaves were supposed to be free over there. If you go up to Canaan Land, someone told us, you are free on the spot, just like those people in the Bible. I wondered how it happened, how you got from a slave to a free person. Was there a borderline you passed through, cutting you from the past and pushing you straight into the future?

All I wanted was to get going again, headed to safety across this river. Grandpa didn't say much about it now. He hardly spoke, as if each word was too heavy to say. Always, before resting, he'd whisper stories about the other side. I'd fall asleep to his words. Maybe Grandpa was hurting too bad. But ever since we jumped out of that wagon, Grandpa suddenly stopped talking about Canada. He never even turned his head to study the opposite side of the river and wonder about it the way I did. Couldn't he hear it talking to us? The other side was calling us to come over.

Finally, when it was no longer deep dark, my thoughts couldn't circle around anymore. I fell asleep. Still no sign of Levi.

Chapter 5
THE GRANDPA I KNEW

COME FIRST LIGHT AND WITH IT, Levi's flat step. I could feel him running right through the ground as I rested my cheek upon it. It shook me awake. Grandpa and I both shot our heads up.

"Get down. Go back to sleep," he ordered us. "Wake me at dusk if it's quiet on the road. Don't wait 'til dark."

Grandpa asked, "What you hear at that church?"

Levi got busy digging himself into a hole on the side of the hill beneath a pine tree, stirring up a mess of dry branches to bed beneath. He disappeared from sight, leaving the two of us staring at leaves. Again Grandpa asked and again we got silence. So we let him be.

But I got to thinking how Levi refused to let me go with him last night. All those hours he'd been gone away from us. Enough time to make plans of his own. I remembered how he was ready to jump off the wagon and leave us behind. What if he left us now? There'd be no one to help with Grandpa. We'd be on our own.

Beside me, Grandpa turned over with a gasp. Seemed like something cut off his breath. All that pain he had and I could do nothing. Then I remembered the beef jerky and handed him a piece. His dark eyes lit for the first time in days.

"You saved this all night?" He grinned and set the piece inside his mouth. "Gettin' to be like your grandpa, squirrelin' stuff away."

23

He lay back, settled on his back again, and grew quiet. We slept most of that day, on and off. But not too deep. Someone had to be on guard. Someone had to wake us to hear Levi's story.

Grandpa was the one to call us. Levi crawled over, taking care to move quiet. He went straight to look at Grandpa's foot. It was still swollen. Looked like it was on sideways with that ankle bone sticking out. But when we tried helping him up to soak it in the river, Grandpa couldn't sit up. His mouth opened wide as he rubbed his right hip bone. A look passed between Levi and Grandpa, but no words.

"Up at that Baptist Church, there's room for one more in their cellar hideaway," said Levi. "They shelter runaways. Got a full house. One woman's about to give birth and all her family is with her."

"Sound like good people," Grandpa said.

"Some of the folks runnin' that church and depot are free. Some are runaways. Said they'd feed you and set your ankle both."

Grandpa's eyes opened wide. He looked around like he couldn't believe his ears.

"Such a place I've been layin' here prayin' for."

Levi unwrapped a cloth bundle on the ground. Cooked oatmeal. Slices of potato. Salt pork. We dug in with our fingers. The food was long cold but it slipped down our throats easy as grease. I licked the last crumb on the cloth clean.

Food sinking down into my belly made me bold. I dared ask what was burning up in me all day long as I lay in the leaves like my whole body was on fire. "What about *us*, Levi? Where we gonna hide while Grandpa heals?"

Levi turned to Grandpa, ignoring me. "Church folks said

there's a crossin' place nearby, upriver, just like I hoped. The current slows down there and it's only a half mile or so across."

"When are you thinkin' of crossin' over?" asked Grandpa.

Levi leaned close to Grandpa. "Slavecatchers already stopped by, askin' for me, those folks warned. Rumours around town about two men snooping around, probably on a slave's trail. They get a big reward if they catch me. I got no choice but to cross over tonight."

"So soon?" Grandpa gasped. "Where can you go from here? How will you be safe?"

"Slavecatchers roam that town too — Fort Erie, across the river in Canada. So the church is sendin' me to a big house over there, one with white pillars. Call it Bertie Hall. Got a tunnel that leads from the river into its cellar. It's one of the last depots on the underground."

I shivered. I thought you could put on freedom like a set of new clothes once you crossed over, but it wasn't like that at all. Those drivers were still after us. Even on the other side, we wouldn't be safe. Whatever trouble Levi was in, it sure followed our trail. The other slaves at home had been right all along about him.

"But how do you get across?" Grandpa asked.

"If one of the men from Bertie Hall is sailin' their boat tonight, I can get aboard. They stop on this side all the time to pick up smuggled goods. Carry runaways too. Smugglers' boats, they told me, flash signals — three lights blinkin' . . . a pause . . . then three more."

"And if they don't show tonight?"

"Then I'll swim across."

Nobody said anything about where I'd be going. Only one place I wanted to be — with Grandpa.

Grandpa finally looked at me. "My mind is set. I'm goin' to the church. And Solomon is travellin' ahead with Levi. I didn't run these months and risk our lives for my grandson to hole up on this side."

My stomach set to twirling like those river waters. For the first time in my life, I thought Grandpa was dead wrong. Everything he said up until that moment made sense. Everything he had told me before, I obeyed. I stood straight up and slammed my fists into the nearest tree.

"No!" I hissed. "I'm not goin' without you. I'll stay behind in these woods until you get better."

Grandpa shook his head. When he spoke, his whole mouth sagged, so that he looked like the old ones back on the plantation instead of the grandpa I knew. "No tellin' how long I'll be. But I promise we'll meet up on the other side."

Levi shot Grandpa a look. Cold and silent, it set the shivers right through me.

"Soon as I can, I'll follow you," Grandpa said, his eyes darting back and forth between Levi and me. "Just leave word at that hall about where you're goin'."

I stood fast by the tree.

"Got no time to fight you, Solomon. It's already dark," Levi said as he looked around. "We got to bring your grandpa to hidin' and cross this river tonight. You gonna help or do I leave you here, all alone?"

My heart jumped out of my chest when he said that. I scrambled back to them, helping Grandpa up, pushing his body straight onto Levi's stooped shoulders. We moved swift and soundless, just us two rushing over the ground. All the while, Grandpa breathed harder than us, panting. I never ran like that before, wanting to disappear, even wishing Grandpa and I were back in the South, side by side in the fields. At least we were together there. All those months on the underground road, nothing separated us. So much I had to say to Grandpa, all of it sinking down deep in my stomach, far out of reach.

At last we squatted in some bushes along a dark street. A church was nearby, tall and red, a dim light in the basement window. Levi grabbed two twisted sticks and handed them to Grandpa.

"Think you can lean on these to get to the back of the church on your own, Jacob? We can't be seen with you. Someone may be watchin'."

Grandpa took a stick in each hand and stood up best he could, half bent over. He didn't have far to go — across a path, behind the church, then down into the cellar where someone said they'd be waiting.

He turned to Levi. "You remember the reason I ran? This boy got to have a better life. Soon as you are settled in one place, he goes to school. Be true to my plans."

Levi patted Grandpa's back. "Rest easy, Jacob. I'll take care of him."

I was standing right by his elbow, like always, my chin lifted up, listening to his every word, when Grandpa pulled me close.

"You obey all Levi says. It won't be easy at first. Go to school. Do the chores he sets. When I come, it'll make me proud to see what you have done."

He pressed me into his chest hard enough for me to feel his heart pumping slow and heavy like drumbeats. Then he let me go. I went whirling back into nothingness, nothing to hold me up anymore. Just a huge lump in my throat where the words should have been. I needed to say something fast about when we'd meet up and where and let him know I'd wait and wait for him at Bertie Hall. But my lips pressed together hard and flat and did not move at all.

Grandpa hobbled away slow, pressing on his good side to steady himself. By the edge of the church, he stopped. But he did not turn around. I will always remember that. He lifted one hand high in the air, held it there a long minute, and disappeared around the back.

We watched and waited. Dim candlelight glowed through the cellar toward the back of the church and then crossed back into it again, wavering. Shadows of two men side by side appeared. Someone held onto Grandpa. They'd take care of him now. He was safe inside. I leaned there like a tree. I could have watched all night long.

Levi called me to go, hissing in my ear. "You hear me, Solomon? Let's go!"

That's when I came to. An awful screaming was building up inside but I could not let it out. All those words I never said to Grandpa and now it was too late. Not even a goodbye had I whispered to him. It felt like all my guts were falling down out of me onto the ground. I don't know if I fell or crawled off or what I did. All I remember is Levi heaving me onto his shoulders like a sack of potatoes and running hard back to the river, me kicking and squirming the whole way. If only he hadn't held on so tight; if only he wasn't so oxen strong, I would have got loose and run all the way back to Grandpa Jacob.

Chapter 6
BETWEEN HERE AND THERE

BY THE TIME WE GOT TO THE RIVERBANK, the moon was no longer high but already sinking. It was long past midnight. Levi had set me down some distance back, but held tight to my wrist, yanking me through the woods. My body argued with him, fighting his strength, squirming away as he pulled me ahead, like a tug-of-war.

He won, like always. I was so tired out by then, felt like I was sleepwalking.

By the shore, we lay flat beneath some willows and looked out. One big sailing boat floated far upriver. Another tied to the shore. Smokestacks upriver. No smuggler's boat waiting for us like we hoped, hidden in the bushes as Levi'd been told. Straight across, two white pillars shone on a house high above the riverbank, at the last depot, Bertie Hall.

And the ink-black river running between us.

"We gotta swim. Hop on. Ride on my back all the way," Levi told me. "Hold on real tight. Don't let go. Keep your feet kickin' water along with mine."

I looked at the water. Shivery cold. Pieces of wood bobbed up and down. Some of it sunk and drowned or passed by so quick with the current pulling it downriver. How could I dare go into it? I shook my head and squatted down on the ground. My face was wet with tears and river spray.

"You got to do this, Solomon. I'll take you over safe to

the other side, just like I promised your grandpa."

My whole body quivered. Since I came into the world, one person was always there. Grandpa made all the decisions: when to plant collards, when to pick them, and when to light out with Levi on the underground road. Nothing I ever did between waking and sleeping was without him by my side. How could I step into those dark waters without him and leave him behind? My legs felt like willow branches, thin and wobbly. Worries buzzed in my head like a nest of swirling yellowjackets.

"You think your grandpa would have let you loose with me unless he believed I could take you across? That's all he wanted — for you to be free."

He stepped into the river and moved ahead without me. My feet sank into the mud at the river's edge. I set one toe in. The cold water grabbed my breath away. I gasped for air. But Levi wasn't waiting, so I stepped in and followed him. When the water touched my chest, I reached out both hands and wrapped myself around Levi's neck like he was a boat. I lay flat on his back. He lifted one arm high and then the next and started to swim across the water. But after every few strokes ahead, we drifted some downriver, away from the far bank, away from the gleaming white pillars.

Soon he couldn't talk to me anymore. His breath came rasping. His arms beat the water faster and faster. I knew I should do something. Kick, he had said. But I was frozen stiff on his back.

Things sailed by. Branches. Leaves. But when the rotten log floated past so swift with something on top of it, Levi stopped swimming. We both stared at it. On the back of the log clung a dirty grey shirt. We turned our heads all around. Nobody upstream; nobody downstream. Whoever had clung to that log was long gone. Or dead. When we looked ahead again, we saw how we drifted downriver too far. On the opposite bank, a distance upstream, a lantern flashed: one, two jolts of light, two times. The wrong signal. We'd been warned about smugglers and customs agents, both ready to turn us in.

Levi beat hard against the current, away from the lights, but he didn't move ahead. He fought the current again and suddenly both our heads dunked under. We bobbed up like apples and spit out dark water. We were in the very middle of the river, in the coldest, deepest part where the current ran wild and swift. My legs began to tremble, and then my arms. That set my teeth chattering. Who knows how deep that water was below us. The shore seemed farther and farther away. We were caught between here and there.

My whole body went still, remembering.

I saw it clear. That March night by the stream, sucking reeds with our heads down under the water. My lungs filled with air, not choked with water like I feared. Drumming on the ground above, all those horses' hooves driving after us as we slipped into the water, covering ourselves beneath it like a blanket. Hunting horns calling everyone to the chase. Hounds yelping without stop, wild with our scent.

There was a reason I sank into an ice-cold stream that night, frost sprinkled over the fields. It was Grandpa who went down in first, though he feared water, while Levi showed me silently how to use the reed. I went down because Grandpa was somehow breathing below the water with such a reed in his mouth. I sunk down beside him easy as eating sweet corn.

I shut my eyes tight, looking back, and begged Grandpa to tell me how to cross *this* river. I even saw us back in the reeds, sucking air to stay alive while those hounds stopped close to the water's edge and howled like a murder was gonna happen. But by the time those slavecatchers caught up with them, we heard them curse their dogs, yanking them away, for leading them astray.

A full deep breath filled my lungs. My head was above water now and Grandpa had told me I was strong enough to run the underground. So I stretched out my legs into the cold river and thrashed my feet hard. Levi's feet answered mine in return. The two of us were fighting strong, slapping harder and harder against the current. I could hear Levi panting like he was running hard. I kicked and kicked, half rabbit, half frog, slamming my feet against the South behind us.

And then Grandpa's laughter came rippling over that water into my ears.

"Right in front of their noses!" he had joked. "We were right there down in the water and they couldn't see us. Fooled 'em good."

How he had chuckled about the reeds. For days afterwards, he kept slapping his leg and talking about it. All I had to do was look at him and he'd grin back, remembering how we got through easy.

See, I thought, *he's with me now, crossin' over. We're carryin' him on our backs. He's comin' with us.*

That's how I floated across to the other side.

Chapter 7
STEPPING INTO THE SHADOWS

LEVI FELL ONTO THE BANK of the Niagara River. Flat to the mud, his chest heaving, sucking at air like he couldn't find any. Our clothes clung to our bodies as we lay out there in the open where anyone could find us. We couldn't get up. Chills ran up and down our bodies, setting our bones to quivering. Never before had I seen Levi like this.

So I poked him. Not hard. Just enough to remind him I was still here. "We are on the other side. Got to hide. Otherwise we won't be safe."

He gasped. "How long have I been lyin' here?"

I shrugged. "Don't know. But I'm freezin' through and through. Let's go."

We crawled for a time, squeezing close to the riverbank below tall trees. A road was in the distance. The moon disappeared. Finally white pillars shone directly above us, with a big house behind them.

"We can't be seen comin' out of this river. Supposed to be a tunnel here. Let's find it."

Everywhere, bushes, pieces of old boats and decaying logs covered the ground. We searched upstream and downstream and still could find no tunnel. We rubbed our arms and legs up and down to keep the chill off.

Then the dark shifted ever so slight. It was coming on first light soon. Levi immediately turned to the bushes on the bank beneath the house, right in line with the pillars. He set to digging leaves and gathering branches to hide beneath. I dug beside him. Suddenly his hand hit something hard. We swept away the branches and there, in the side of the hill, was a metal handle. Around it was stone. A door.

I stood back as Levi first pushed, then heaved on it. It opened a crack, enough for us to see what was behind it. A deep black cave stinking of wetness. Stone walls, high and wide. Moss creeping all over it. Water marks up to the ceiling like it had flooded over many times. Some wooden crates piled to one side.

Behind us, the sky was opening pink and light. Levi pushed me inside the tunnel first, then himself, tugging the door shut behind us. Inside was blacker than night. On both sides of us, the walls were thick with beads of water. Levi stepped ahead and I followed. The icy air was so foul and musty, I didn't dare breathe. It stunk of rot.

We seemed to be walking underneath the hill. Gusts of air rushed at us from the sides, maybe from empty spaces. Levi stopped dead in front of me.

I bumped into him and felt him turn toward the right, then the left. Winds swirled like a storm brewing. It blew underneath my clothes and raised goosebumps all over my skin. My wet pants clung to my legs like ice fingers. I didn't dare breathe. Something was coming toward us. I grabbed Levi's shirt in both hands and held on.

Then I saw it straight on.

A shadow blocked the way ahead. It wavered back and forth like candlelight. Then it came into view. A boy, thin, and so pale I could see *through* him.

A scream rose in my throat. I turned away to run back to

the river, out of this cramped tunnel, but Levi grabbed me. I was stuck between the two of them.

"What's got into you, Solomon? We got to go ahead. Back there is daylight."

I whirled around. The boy drifted like smoke, his dark eyes lighting on me like he was eating me up. I stared at him and Levi stared at me.

"You don't *see* him?" I asked.

"What's there to see? It's pitch black in here."

I sank right down. I couldn't step ahead and I couldn't go back. I couldn't see Levi, but I did see this boy in front of me: a white boy in a fancy Sunday suit, suspenders holding up his pants. He stepped closer now, filling the tunnel from side to side with fog.

We could not pass.

I looked closer at the boy. Flashes of the other side of the tunnel appeared through his body.

The old ones, the bent-over men back on the plantation who couldn't work anymore, who just sat and whittled wood all day, say darkness draws more evil to you. Like how I was sick with grief over leaving Grandpa behind. Full of such worry, I felt like I could lie down and give up. I had stepped into shadows. That's how this boy found me. He sniffed my deep-down sorrow. It matched his own mood.

This boy was a ghost.

Then he started murmuring words like someone breathing inside my head. "No boy plays here anymore. My father forbids it."

Here was a boy. Or what was once a boy. He wasn't alive though. No white boy was gonna tell me what to do anymore. He was not an elder. I wasn't going to be bossed by him like I'd been bossed all my life. Not after those months of running scared. Not in this dark place. I wanted to run through there fast. So I began to talk to him, the way I learned with Grandpa all those years the overseer watched us. Not with my mouth, but silently, from inside my own head.

"I'm not playin'. Just passin' through On my way to freedom."

"Freedom? There's no freedom here without a body."

"Freedom is here for me — on this side, where I'm not a slave anymore."

"What are you leaving behind? You are running from something, I can tell."

"Sure I'm runnin'," I told him. "From work that never ends. Dawn to dusk hunger. No chance to be myself. And I'm leavin' something precious behind — my own grandpa."

"You want to go on without him?"

How his question shivered through me like my own soul speaking. I had not wished to go ahead and somehow this ghost knew. I stared into its white-rimmed eyes. It was like stepping into another world. . . . A table full of roast turkey and fine china plates . . . Children running by the river . . . Laughter . . . A hide and seek game . . . A smiling mother and father. All he left behind when he entered this tunnel.

I never even dreamed of getting near those things this boy once had. I wondered if this ghost would give me the chance for any of them. So I kept on.

"How did you die?" I asked.

The form wavered as if the memory still hurt. "Drowned. At fourteen. I was playing hide and seek one Easter Day with all my cousins and brothers and sisters. Fell asleep here. Woke to the tunnel flooding over from rivermelt. They sealed the doors on both sides, not knowing I was inside. Now I roam this tunnel, making sure no one plays here like I once did."

With those words, the ghost boy pointed ahead toward the direction of the house and sighed. He couldn't live there anymore, only in this dark, damp tunnel.

"You lost your chance to be free, and I am sorry for that. But will you let us go on ahead? Give me a chance to grow up free. Let us pass."

Silence echoed throughout the tunnel. The ghost shape spread out everywhere, whitening the walls on all sides.

"Rodney was my name. Remember me. How all I wanted was to live and grow up like you. And now I can't."

The boy turned sideways, pressing flat into the wall like vapour.

All the time I lived back home, I felt just like this ghost, more dead than alive. And I knew I had to step deeper into the tunnel. Levi was right. I had to do it without Grandpa. My body rose up.

The boy vanished.

Levi's voice cut clear across to my ears, echoing down the stone walls. "You got over it, boy? This tunnel sure is pressin' us in. Can't breathe inside here. Let's move on."

We kept our hands on one side, following the cool stone ahead.

Suddenly Levi stopped short. "Can't go farther. There's a dead end here."

In the dark, we both kneeled down, pressing our hands into the darkness ahead. There was a firm wall there.

Levi leaned his ear against it. "Nothin'. Gonna try the signal."

He knocked the way he'd been taught. Three hard knocks

and one light one, three times. Code of the underground. Afterwards, we both set our ears to the spot and waited. Nothing. Down the tunnel, water dripped. The far-off echo of the river roared.

"A door!" I remembered what the boy had said. "Maybe it's another door."

Levi stood up. He leaned his body full strength to the wall and I joined in, both of us pushing. Something was shifting. Something was giving way. Such a squeaking, I thought the whole of Fort Erie would hear us. We both stumbled through a door creaking on its rusty hinges to open into a small underground room.

It was drier inside but still cold. A small high window let in some light. So high the ceiling rose above our heads, it seemed a mile up. Levi shut the door to the tunnel. We tiptoed inside. In one corner, hundreds of wooden crates were stacked. Pictures of salt and tea on some boxes. Bottles of liquor too. Some empty cots waited with woollen blankets.

As we moved around the room, every sound kicked off echoes. The inner wall facing us had wooden shelves from floor to ceiling, filled with nails and carpentry tools. All this way we had travelled and now we came into this one small room with just us in it.

Levi kept staring all around until the biggest grin lit his face. He looked ready to dance, to sing, to shout. What he did surprised me. He kneeled down by one of the cots and bowed his head. I knew he was flying up to heaven somewhere, busting with thanks.

"We are on the other side. Safe. With all our lives before us," I heard him pray. "Our bodies are still whole. And our minds will be, soon. Praise God."

But I did not join him. My mind was not free at all. A ghost had brushed against me, reminding me of death and forever-lost chances. Though Grandpa had appeared on the water, breathing his strength into us, he was not here with us in this cellar room. He was still in the country that had branded us as slaves. I huddled alone on the other cot, shaking and wet beneath the woollen blanket, thinking how I came into Canada with only half of myself free. The rest of me stayed behind on the other side.

Chapter 8
UNDERGROUND AT BERTIE HALL

WHEN I AWOKE, IT WAS SHIVERY, the kind of cold you feel in your bones. June sun had shone on top of my head a few days ago. Yet now we were trapped underground. A cold winter day at home felt like this. Except there was always light there. Here it felt like we were buried alive in a cave.

We could not turn back. Or go anywhere except into that tunnel. I dared not set foot in there again. Every time my eyes closed during the night, I popped them open to watch the door to the tunnel.

Levi was awake now too, scratching his head and staring all around. He had slept deep. I was sure about that. I had been wide-eyed listening to his snores for hours. He was just about to say something when we heard a slamming sound way off. Echoes rang behind the inner wall. Footsteps shook the ground floor.

Levi jumped up and headed to the tunnel door. But I sat stiffly on my cot. He jerked his head for me to follow him. His hands grabbed the tunnel door, prying it open. All night long I feared that ghost would push through the door. Instead, there was something coming the other way toward us. We were caught between them. I had no choice but to edge over to Levi's side.

Seemed the whole room started shaking then. The shelves rattled and began sliding away. Nails and hammers clanged to the floor. The whole *wall* was moving. We stood by the tunnel door, ready to run. The breeze from inside blew against my skin, a dank smell. Levi headed into the tunnel and grabbed my arm. Then we heard the words.

"Is anyone in there?" called a weak voice. "I came to check. Don't be afraid!" A wrinkled white face peeked around the shelves, letting light in. A man, white-haired and bent, stood there carrying a candle. The way he bowed his head and his simple, clean clothes, made me guess he was a servant.

"Runaways! Welcome. You've reached safety here at Bertie Hall. I'll go up and tell the owner of the house you have arrived. Sit down now. I'll return with breakfast."

Levi studied his face. Then he looked beyond, into the huge cellar. No one was there. When the servant disappeared, Levi pushed me back inside the small room. The two of us stared at one another but did not speak. My mind was full of a million questions. *Is it safe to linger here? Should we run while he's gone?* Levi sank onto his cot and I plunked down right beside him. As we waited in our hideaway, I peeked into the main cellar. That room was huge and drafty. Far off were stairs leading up and up. I huddled in the blankets and waited some more.

When we heard banging and voices, we shot up and rushed to the tunnel door at the back of the hidden room. Shadows moved across the dim cellar. Footsteps shuffled against the dirt floor, coming closer. The servant entered our small room with a tray of food. Steam blew from a teapot. My stomach knotted up.

"Porridge. Milk. Apples. Bacon and English tea." He set the tray down on a cot.

"Welcome," boomed a voice right behind him. "Sarah Forsyth's my name. My late husband's family traded goods from Buffalo. And gave slaves safety. So I do the same, though both might bring me trouble from the law."

She wore a long grey dress that matched her hair. Bright jewellery shone at her neck and on her fingers. Such finery I had seen back home on the plantation. She must be mistress of the place. Both of us looked down at the floor, not into her eyes. For the woman was white and she was speaking directly to us.

"So young you both are to have taken such a long and dangerous journey. And survived it. You must be starving and cold. Are you well?"

Levi nodded. "There were three of us on the road, ma'am. Jacob's behind on the opposite shore, with injuries. He was the boy's grandpa, his only family."

My head shot up. Missus Forsyth was looking directly at me.

"There must be such an ache in your heart to leave your grandpa behind. May God give you courage to go ahead. Does this man Jacob know to come here?"

Again Levi nodded. I did not dare speak.

"Then Jacob will join you as soon as he can. Now, come and eat, both of you."

Levi began spooning hot porridge into his mouth. All the while, he stood up. I sat down and sipped black tea, letting its heat touch all the cold places inside, places frozen by river and hounds, running and hiding.

"So many runaway slaves have come through here, hundreds since 1850. All go on to new lives. What I would give to see your faces a year from now — full of glory, they'd be. But no one returns here. The whole country lies before you like a promise."

"What is it like here?" Levi whispered, so low it was hard to hear him.

"It depends where you go. Just like anywhere else, you will meet those who have sympathy for runaways. Many abolitionists work in Canada to end slavery in the South. Indeed, our government has invited you to come. But here and there, in places, some may not be ready to welcome you."

"Then where can we go?" asked Levi.

"To a community of coloured people. It's nearby. You'll be free there. You can walk in daylight. Work and make money. Go to church and gain an education."

Levi had gobbled more than half the food when he finally raised his eyes. I grabbed the rest quick, shoved it in my mouth and swallowed in gulps without chewing.

"You mean we can start a new life here?" Levi asked. "Right away?"

"Certainly. You'll be led there before dawn tomorrow. In this land, there are no slaves. Only those who are free."

"Be no trouble?"

"Slavecatchers sometimes dare cross into Canada to chase former slaves — it's outrageous, but it still happens even though we have laws against it here. There's no taking slaves back unless they committed a crime back home. So just in case anyone's watching, or plans on stealing runaways for a reward, we come and go at Bertie Hall only at night, so no one suspects what we do here."

A look passed over Levi's face. It was something I'd seen before, like someone slapped him. It was how he looked when I told him in the back of the wagon about the drivers seeking reward money for him.

"Why do you risk so much, ma'am?" Levi asked Missus Forsyth.

"This river's been our livelihood and sorrow both. Lost my

husband to it. He drowned on the river. My brother-in-law Rodney drowned in this tunnel as a boy. It was sealed over afterwards by my grieving father-in-law. Runaways kept showing up. One was captured nearby. So I opened the tunnel again. And when I did, it felt like my family came back to me. Couldn't save *them*, but I can help you."

Rodney. The name shivered through me. He had stood between me and safety and let me pass. How he must have longed to follow me back home to Bertie Hall.

"Rest now. My servant will bring you clothes. We'll wake you tonight. You'll head straight to Little Africa, a short ride away."

After the servant brought dry clothes, the two sealed our room behind the wall of shelves again. All was quiet and dim, although somewhere outside, it must be daylight. How I wished to get to it, to feel the June sun on my face again, the first sunshine of freedom. I talked up a storm then, asking Levi how it was going to be and what we'd do first. All we did was talk.

"Bet Little Africa is bigger than a plantation!" I burst out. "What do you think?"

Levi threw back his head and laughed. "Talk comes easy when your belly's full."

And then the biggest yawns took us over. Some quivered from my toes all the way up to my ears. I roared them out of my mouth like a lion. We even had a contest over whose yawn lasted longest and loudest. Of course Levi's was the loudest. His mouth was a whole lot bigger than mine.

Afterwards, Levi dropped dead asleep in the middle of talking to me. He didn't even snore. The sound of water dripping somewhere in the tunnel filled the room.

This was my last chance. I had to make sure of something before we left.

Though I did not wish to see the ghost again or call him up out of the tunnel, I had to tell him something. All those words I couldn't tell Grandpa. Now was my chance to speak up. My fingers pried at the door inch by inch so as not to make a sound until I could slip through it sideways. One foot I stuck right behind me in the doorway; the other stepped into darkness.

Couldn't see anything ahead. So damp in there, felt like it was raining. Cool and drafty, it set my throat to tickling. There was a smell of dirt and worms and living below the ground like in some grave.

Then the temperature dropped. Sudden. As if it turned from summer to winter in a moment. The back of my neck felt icy cold. I stepped my foot backwards to stand in the doorway, the heavy door cracked open between both feet. Not one more second did I want to stay in that tunnel.

I faced the dark and said my words silently to Rodney. "You heard me speak of leavin' my grandpa behind. He'll be comin' through when he's healed up. I beg you not to show your face to him. He's too old for such a sight. And . . . please . . , Rodney . . . let him pass through safe, like you did us."

That was enough for me. Didn't wait for an answer. I stepped back into the cellar and heaved that door shut with all my might. Then I slept at last. One long yawn before I fell into the first deep sleep of freedom.

Chapter 9
LITTLE AFRICA, FORT ERIE

WE LAY FLAT IN THE BACK OF THE WAGON, like on so many trips we had taken on the underground road. In the dark, I couldn't help but wonder how in this new land where they said we'd be free, we were still hiding. And I was still holding my breath waiting for the moment when freedom would happen.

The night air was warm though. I wanted this to be the best place, like Missus Forsyth said. I had her promise before we left and I held on tight to her words.

"I'll let your Grandpa Jacob know where you've gone as soon as he crosses," she had said. "Meanwhile, you can live and work in safety until he joins you."

Our driver dropped us in a clearing that he whispered was Little Africa. Levi and I stood together and watched the last stars fade and the treetops appear like shadows. All around us in every direction was forest. Big trees riding straight up to the sky. We were surrounded by them. Not one person. Not one house. Only trees stood there as if guarding us, holding us safe as secrets inside this new country.

The sky took on blue. It was coming on sun-up. Levi and I stared at one another. Seemed the light was all around now, shining outside and inside us too. Warm and bright, sunbeams tunnelled through the trees to touch our faces. Felt we could lift up soft as feathers and float. This was free ground and we stood upon it in daylight for the first time. One loud gasp blew out of me. Levi slapped his legs. Looked like he was working up a shout.

All I could do was spin in circles.

Was I living on the same earth I'd been born on? No! This must be some other place, dropped down from heaven. When we crossed over, we must have come into Canaan, the place that folks whispered about back home. Paradise, they said. Like when the world was first made. I never imagined it would be so green.

We carried on for some time. I'd been stepping lightly, so I knew it wasn't me when, underneath us, the ground shook with stomping feet. We heard them coming long before we saw them. Hid behind some trees until they walked by. Men stepped out of the woods, dark faces grinning, more men than I could count.

"Two new ones!" they shouted. "Lookin' green as the trees."

Big rumbling laughter from the men. We stepped back into the clearing to join them.

"Mornin'! You just crossed?" someone said. "Sure is somethin' to first come here from the other side. We remember that day well. Some of us were once runaways too. Best you wait on our boss, John Bright. He'll be along soon."

More men passed by, enough to fill the whole Tiller plantation. How could we have travelled so far, all those hundreds of miles, only to find a work gang, just like in Georgia? Workers carried tools, saws, axes and tarp. Some heaved water jugs on their shoulders. Some even sang a work song I knew from the cotton fields back home: *Wouldn't drive so hard but . . . I need your arms!*

Then out stepped an older man. Face full of lines, arms full of muscles, he held himself tall. Soon as he saw us, he stopped.

"Welcome!" he said. "You plan on stayin' here with us?"

Levi gasped. "Are you the boss around here?"

The man began to laugh, with such a booming sound you could hear it echo all through the trees. Nobody I knew had ever laughed like that, from deep in their belly, with a rumble so loud the leaves around us were shaking. The two of us stood wide-eyed staring at him. He looked like one of the elders back home, yet here he was in charge of the whole place.

"John Bright's the name. Some call me boss of these woods. But I'm just a go-between. The Kival brothers run the loggin' here. They get orders from ships, railroads, common folk and house builders about who needs what cut. Black walnut. Or hickory. Oak. Maple or ash. It all grows here in plenty. I get the wood ready for 'em all."

"Will you hire us?" Levi asked. "And are you payin' workers?"

Again John Bright laughed. "Think you work for nothin' here? Since the War of 1812 ended, I been workin' and savin' and you will too. Own my own farm now. Seventy cents a day, I'll pay you. For the boy, ten cents. You both got jobs here."

Levi and I gasped. He and John Bright shook hands. Just like that, a plan showed up like summer rain, a quick surprise. Missus Forsyth was true to her word about finding work here. It meant she could be counted on to look out for Grandpa too.

"All right, then. You gonna need to set up a place to sleep. We got tarp for tents. And no workin' here without heavy boots. Go see Charley over in the village and he'll get you settled. Soon as he does, he'll show you where the men are at today."

Levi's feet shot out to find Charley after John gave directions, and for once I was right beside him. We stopped at a crossroads where there was a church and a store. John had said that behind it lay cemetery grounds already filling with those who had been crossing into Canada in great numbers since 1793. Some greying wooden crosses stood up in one corner. And a fresh mound of dirt with no marking. Some folks had died of starvation or disease shortly after they arrived, we were told; others had worked here and grown old. It made me quiver to see the dead so close to the living. Grannie, who believed in all kinds of superstitions, had warned me about being too near the dead. I promised her never to step foot in such a place. Ever. It surely must be haunted.

I was glad to step into the shop. Inside, wooden shelves were filled with rows and rows of boots. Jeans. Rope. Dried beans. Cornmeal in barrels. Beef jerky hanging in strips. In the back, a shoemaker cut leather strips for boots.

Charley, the shopkeeper, looked Levi and me up and down. "Growin' men tall as trees down South, I see," he said. "And bringin' over young ones to live in our village. Let's see what I got to fit you both."

By the time Charley was done, we both wore hard-used leather boots, not like the thin shoes we had back home. He pointed out a spot to set up our tent, then gave us pots and some cornmeal, along with a water jug. Our first week's earnings would pay for these things, he told us. I kept looking down at my boots all that day. After all that running from the South, it sure felt good to step down in something so firm. Charley said we would soon find out why we had to wear such heavy boots. As we headed into the woods, everywhere on the ground were broken branches, cut wood, splinters and sawdust.

In the middle of the woods, we came upon a gang of men at work. Some trimmed branches off fallen trees. Others stood right on top of whole logs, breaking them into chunks, flinging axes high above their heads and landing them square down on the wood. All you heard was the chopping and slamming of wood.

"This wood will be fuel for the ships' furnaces to burn," John Bright said. "So they can ferry across Lake Erie and along the Niagara River." We watched the men. Nobody was shouting orders or cursing or shoving anybody. Though the men called directions to one another, they joked too. There seemed to be no overseer lurking at all. No Master either. No whips hanging from belts. No pistols tucked into waists. Everybody was busy and constantly moving. And nobody watched with narrowed eyes and folded arms. How did it run by itself?

"Hey, you!" yelled a worker to Levi. "You any good with a double-bitted axe?"

Levi started grinning at once. He stood tall with his feet planted wide apart. I believe he was puffing his chest up too. He had grown up axing brush and trees down.

"Toss it over!" he called back.

The axe whirred through the air in his direction. I leaped out of the way. Levi shot his hand out and grabbed it safely by the wooden handle. Most stayed clear of such an axe, for it had sharp blades at either side. Likely to whack someone in back of you too when you use it. But in Levi's hands that axe was already swinging above his head in circles as he warmed up. He shifted his weight around on both hips until he finally found the right spot to stand. Workers nearby stood watching him. *Slam!* The axe fell into a fallen chunk of log. A crack yawned wide open in it. Three more slams and it broke into two pieces.

Somebody whistled. John Bright set his hands on his hips and nodded.

"Guess he's got the job all right!" one man laughed.

Levi caught me leaning in toward him with my eyes big. "You wanna help out?"

I rushed over, fitting in beside him like I used to do with Grandpa. Only now, it was Levi swinging the axe and me scrambling to collect the pieces that zinged through the air and fell to the ground with a smack. We soon built up a cord of firewood beside all the other piles the loggers made. The biggest grins lit up both our faces. We were a team. Hard to keep up with Levi though. I was panting.

Levi was right at home here in these woods that stretched higher and wider than any we'd known before. We had run those hundreds of miles, never knowing what was ahead, never guessing what a free country would be like, only to find that a place like Canaan was waiting for us. Axing trees down was work Levi had done back home. But he would be working for *himself* now. No one would be pushing him. The wonder of it made my mouth drop.

Just then, a far-off whistle blew, chugging and tooting in the distance. I stopped working to listen. Back home, I'd heard trains from far, far away. Their low whistle was so lonesome sounding, especially if you heard it at night. Seemed like someone endlessly crying. But the train in Canada did not sound like that all. It shouted loud and bold as a crow about how's it's rushing across free land. This train was in such a hurry to get places straight away, it made my heart flip. Maybe, just maybe, it'd take me with it someday.

"Hear that train?" John asked. "It runs clear across the belly of this country from one great lake to another. That's the Buffalo and Lake Huron leavin' Fort Erie. Railways buy our wood too. They are buildin' rails everywhere around Little Africa. A cord of our wood keeps those trains travellin' fifty miles an hour. Nothin' faster than that."

Never had I imagined anything could zoom past at that

51

speed. I'd sure keep watch for a train to see if it was true. I promised myself that I would give a listen to all its comings and goings each and every day, hoping to catch a glimpse. All I wanted was to see a real train face to face.

I turned in circles, taking it all in. This small village of Little Africa was its own free country. Full of everything we needed to live. Work right in front of us. Money to save up. I'd already startled up a pheasant, and rabbits were everywhere if we were lucky enough to catch one to roast. Cool streams trickled in the woods to drink and dunk in. Safe at last. Each part of me pulsed alive. My eyes filled with green. The piney smell of fresh-cut logs filled my nose.

Even my feet felt different in those boots. Freedom was in my feet. That sure is one odd spot to feel it. They rooted me to the ground like some growing thing. Like pails on my feet, my boots forced me to step down heavy. Back on the plantation, I tiptoed, slipping like a shadow so the overseer wouldn't notice me. I was inside myself, floating, back then.

In Little Africa, I began to land down in my own body, pound by pound, as my feet beat the free ground hard.

I am no longer a slave, the message beat out beneath my boots as I ran with armloads of fresh-cut wood to stack on the woodpiles.

I am Solomon, the boy I was meant to be, runnin' across the land of promises.

Chapter 10
STUDYING THE STARS

THE SONG OF THE RAILROAD RUNNING was the first sound that woke me every morning and its shrill whistle was the last sound I heard before falling asleep. In between those sounds was work among the trees.

Everywhere in Little Africa were fallen logs. Lumber of all shapes and sizes. Men were opening wide pathways in the forest where once many trees had grown. Huge stumps were all that spoke of a tree once growing there. Levi set to work at once carting fallen trees to a spot where workers were hauling them north to the Falls. Soon, he was loading cut wood onto wagons. Then Levi was gone whole afternoons, in and out of the forest, somewhere down the Niagara River where a ship waited to carry logs from Canada across to New York. The only time we were together was late in the evenings while we cooked dinner. Though I told him all about my day's work, or how I learned that trains took folks on holiday to see the Falls and wondered if he'd like to go there too, Levi only nodded or said "mmm." Often, by the time we ate our last bite, his head dropped and his eyes shut.

On my first weeks, I stayed behind with the loggers, gawking at first, open-mouthed. They were busy hauling and splitting and chopping. Dangerous work. My job was to clean up after them, clearing the path so we could walk upon it safe. Best not to even face the workers when they chop because splinters fly and poke into your eyes. Once I got whacked in the back by a flying piece of wood.

I tried to help the men, but mostly I got in their way and they ordered me to step back. All my life, I had worked beside Grandpa Jacob. I learned by following him. Now I was on my own. My hands dangled heavy as stumps by my sides. When Levi and I cut and stacked together, we had a rhythm to our work. We'd known each other our whole lives. Now I felt like some slow bumblebee, always in the workers' way.

One morning John Bright appeared early. "Got a new job for you right here," he said. "Firewood boy."

Over and over I bent to the ground, gathering cut pieces of wood strewn everywhere. Some thin slivers for kindling fires I set in one pile. Cordwood got stacked up for burning in fireplaces. No one else short enough to do this job, I guessed. No one wanted to stoop all day and there were no other boys my age here. Best part about my new job was that anyone could ride up to buy kindling and cordwood and they'd have to come to me for help to load it onto their wagon. Charley had told them where I was at.

"Solomon!" white men cried out, looking for me.

Often they were servants. Some sat silent and stiff-backed. But some chatted about the weather and wondered how I liked Canada, and I even spoke a few words back. These men smiled and seemed happy for my crossing over. Sometimes gentlemen sat on board beside them, dressed in grey stripes and felt hats. They always watched the workers closely. I never dared speak to these men. When I was done loading wood, they reached out their gloved hands to slip a copper halfpenny into my hand. I bowed my head in thanks. First time it happened, John Bright winked at me. That's how I knew to keep it secret. I smiled on the inside each time a coin dropped into my pocket.

On June nights, by a campfire that glowed long after dark, after we licked our fingers of the roasted rabbit Levi had trapped, he curled up in the tent and I stretched out on the ground to sleep beneath the stars. Kicked off my boots to let the blisters air. Seemed I had no body left at all. Like I was a fallen log. I fell asleep in an instant.

Then one evening when the nights were getting warmer and the days hotter and we were swatting plenty of mosquitoes, Levi was propped up, eyes still open. He'd been in a shouting match that afternoon with a newly arrived runaway from South Carolina named Hiram. John Bright had to be called in to settle the fight. Levi's jaw seemed locked tight still.

"Suppose you're wonderin'. Hiram was givin' orders and I wouldn't go along. Told him I take orders from no one but the boss. I shouldn't have got so worked up."

"Did John help out?"

"Sure did. Calmed me down. Made it clear he's the boss. I had to apologize. Seems I always lose my temper and fight the way things are. It's all I know how to do. That and runnin'."

Levi never spoke to me much except to give orders. He was never still long enough, I suppose. So I felt I should tell him something now.

"You got us out of slavery safe and sound, Levi. I wouldn't be here 'cept for you. So I got plenty to thank you for."

He stared at me a long time. "Sure I got us here. I'm bullheaded and go after what I want. Been that way all my life. Just like my pa. You remember Enos?"

I nodded. Often on the underground road, I thought back to him. He towered over everyone, but was so slow and silent, like most of him was missing. We never heard him say a word. It was hard to believe he had once been a runaway. Those shackles branded him, a warning to all of us to stay put on the plantation and never even think of running.

"Such a strong man, my pa, and they broke him into pieces. Between whippin' and overworkin', not much left of Enos. Hardly spoke to me in the end. I left without even tellin' him I was runnin'. Afraid they'd beat him to find out what he knew."

I remembered how my pa kept his going away a secret too. We never said goodbye. There'd been no plans to meet up again, nothing to hope for. Perhaps Pa had not told us in order to keep us safe too. His leave-taking was all mixed up in my mind. I was only six then. There'd been blood at the time, I recall, staining the cabin floor. Don't know why. I don't remember if it was a dream or if it was true. How I wished to tell Levi about Pa, but I was too afraid of tears coming. I bit my lips and warned myself to be quiet.

Levi's voice rose up. "Do you know what it's like to see your own pa beaten right in front of you, his ankles chained forever and you can't do anythin'? Nothin'!"

He smacked his fists together and sat up. "I had to do it —"

"Do what?"

"Oh . . . nothin' . . . run, that's all. Good timin' for you and Jacob. Let's just hope he won't be long comin' over. Now let's get some sleep. Maybe livin' longer in freedom will make me go easy. That's what John says."

Levi crawled into the tent. Before he lay down, he said one last thing. "We have to look ahead now. Make a place for ourselves here in Little Africa. Can't look back."

When it got quiet, I looked up at the stars and remembered how this was what Grandpa and I used to do back home after a long day's work. We'd lie flat and look up at the sky. If we had any thoughts, we'd let them free, telling one another everything. I didn't want to give up on Grandpa like Levi had to do with old Enos.

What is Grandpa doing now? We left him just weeks ago and already it felt like a year. Crossing the river had made a cut between us. I didn't know how long he'd take to heal up and walk right again. When I got to thinking that way, my chest began heaving and the sky began swirling so I bit my lips hard and told myself to be still.

I looked up at the treetops, the way their trunks stood tall and straight and how they just waited. They didn't fuss. *Be like these trees*, I told myself, *standing silent. Be still and listen, that's how you learn.* I was so close to where we left Grandpa, maybe I might hear him if I tried. Owls hooted through the trees. Levi did not wake. I pretended to be a tree, forever listening still. Minutes and minutes, I waited.

The voice threaded through the woods and wound its way through my heart. Creaky and slow, it came steady. *I am lyin' on this same ground as you, Solomon. Lookin' up and studyin' these same stars. Just this cold river runnin' between us right now. Won't be for long. Wait on me. I'll cross over and meet you on the other side someday.*

My chest began to fill again, lifting full and wide. Grandpa was nearby after all. I was safe now, I reminded myself. Not looking ahead like we did for four long months, always waiting and hiding, but actually *here*. Working outside all day and sleeping outside at night too, like I always wanted. Levi was right. We had a home in Little Africa. All that could be done now was wait for Grandpa to come over. Meanwhile, all those coins earned would be saved for him and me to settle. There'd been some pennies from rich townsfolk too. That I never told Levi. I got busy planning for Grandpa to come. His first day here, I'd buy him the best pair of boots in Charley's shop. Wouldn't that surprise him? Only the rich wore such fancy boots, he'd always told me, not common folk like us. His eyes would pop wide open when he saw my shiny coins in one hand and the boots in the other. He'd laugh all day long after he put on his first pair of boots and strutted around in them. Bet he'd dance too.

That night, as the last train whistle blew and my eyes shut, I told myself Grandpa Jacob was just a few miles away. He'll be coming over . . . soon. . . . soon . . . soon.

That was the last thought I had before falling asleep each and every night that first summer of freedom in Fort Erie. And I wondered if he heard my voice clear across on the other side like I heard his.

Chapter 11
THE TREES TEACH ME

July 1857

I HAD SPENT MY ELEVEN YEARS with men around me. Here, it was the same. Most were hard-working like Levi, carting wood planks everywhere. Here were many others who had run north like us and plopped down near the border. Over a hundred, I'd been told. All needing money and a job. Tired of running. Mostly it was the young and strong who lived here. Maybe you had to be strong to even think of going all the way to Canada, or else half crazy like we thought Levi was. There were few old folks in Little Africa. Women lived in some of the cabins, carrying babies on their hips or with toddlers grabbing their skirts. Some women sold us dinner if we hadn't snagged a groundhog or raccoon that day.

Drenched in sweat, I was free to run off and hide in the shade to rest, gulp handfuls of creek water, hoot into the woods to set the air echoing, whistle whenever I felt like it. Nobody flicking a whip. I moved in time with the busy men, wood passing from their hands into mine. My woodpile grew in the mornings and shrank in the afternoons. Work songs chanted in my ear. These men gave me Sunday smiles when they sat down to rest beside me, just like the men back home did on the one day they did not work. But here, in Little Africa, men smiled even on workdays.

One July afternoon, after being in Little Africa a month or so, I looked around and realized how different it was here. It wasn't silent like back home in the cotton fields where the most you heard was cricket song come morning or work song come afternoon. From dawn to sundown in Little Africa, shouts startled the air. Trees were falling everywhere, and when they did, loud voices screamed out which way the trunks were dropping.

"Watch your back!" the men warned as I scrambled over the ground for kindling.

"Here's one for you, Johnny!"

"Let 'er rip!"

That day was the first time Levi was put in charge of sawing whole trees down with a partner named Cato. They carried one cross-cut saw between them. At first, some hollering by Cato. But mostly grunting and sawing, pushing and pulling like a tug-of-war between the two of them. The cross-cut saw sliced deeper and deeper through the widest tree until that trunk stood still one heart-thumping moment, held up by a few splinters. Men ran off every which way. Such a silence. Even the birds stopped singing. Then the whole tree smashed flat down with a solid whoosh. The ground shook right through my boots.

"All that axin' back home sure made me strong," Levi said afterwards. "I can saw these trees down with my eyes closed. That's how easy it is."

He was joking of course. Levi always said such things. You don't ever want to shut your eyes or turn your back in a place like Little Africa. The very next day, Cato and Levi were sawing back and forth on a tree and the men standing behind Levi warned us that it was going to drop our way soon. We all scurried off like birds when they smell a hurricane blowing in, because when those sky-high trees fell, they smacked you too if you happened to be nearby. Behind me, I heard that tree quiver round and round until finally it cracked sideways, crushing one man's foot and breaking another man's arm. They never saw it coming.

* * *

Payday was the best day of the whole month, always the second Saturday.

"We are our own masters here," John Bright said as he handed out our money. "This belongs to you. You earned it with your own sweat."

Afterwards, we went back to our tent grinning, our pockets sagging with coins. Levi dug a hole beneath the tarp to hide our earnings. He slept right on top of it like some hound dog over its bone. Each week, he piled up all our coins and asked John Bright how much it made. When John told us we had about five dollars saved that first month, we couldn't believe it. Better than that, for July he gave us a raise: I got fifteen cents for being firewood boy and Levi earned a silver dollar a day for working with the cross-cut saw because it's dangerous work. Between the two of us, our July wages would be twenty-seven dollars and sixty cents. I stashed my extra coins in the woods someplace secret that I didn't even tell Levi about. They were just for Grandpa and me.

Neither of us knew much about money. I remembered Master strutting around when he came back from a slave auction. Whisperings afterwards that Levi's older brother Silas brought four hundred dollars that day. We never saw that boy again. And Levi never spoke of him afterwards, just clenched his fists if you should say his name. Once you were sold, the world swallowed you up. Like you fell down a well. Though four hundred dollars must have been a heap of money, the copper half-penny token that fell into my open hands in Little Africa was much sweeter. For it was all mine.

A few days later, new workers passed through Little Africa, men I never saw before, walking in a long line like a work gang. Some just crossed over that summer and looked raggedy. Others said they've been here a year. John said they were heading to work at Miller's Creek. When they brushed past me, seemed like they were marching to the fields, in such numbers and in such a long line, in the mists of early morning. It set my heart to pumping. I stopped and stared at them. Suddenly, in every face, I looked for one face. *Pa could be among them*, the thought suddenly sprang up, *and I wouldn't even know him.*

It'd been five years since I last saw him. Every time I tried to picture his face, it was blurry. There wasn't anything about him I remembered for sure. The only remembering I had was about blood. It was dripping thick and red on the cabin floor and it could never be scrubbed away afterwards. How could a boy ever forget his own pa's face? Such a thing I wouldn't confess to anyone. So I studied each and every face passing by. Had Pa made it this far north? Did he come this way? I did not know. So many ways to cross the border, I'd been told. But not one face was the one.

No stranger stopped and wondered who I might be, a lone boy belonging to no one. I dared not even hope that somehow Grandpa might pass by too. If I thought about him too much, a big lump would stick in my throat.

* * *

John Bright filled our ears with all kinds of stories. There'd be a holiday coming in August, he said, the one day no man in Little Africa would pick up an axe. Instead, they'd celebrate their freedom from slavery with a parade. Levi and I stared at each other when he said that. Could we really march like he said and sing out in the open right in front of rich white people and not keep to ourselves in the village of Little Africa? Of course we'd had celebrations back home, but they were at Christmas or harvest time when most of the work was done, not smack in the middle of summer. That's when Mingo played the fiddle and young couples danced by firelight. Knee clapping, spoons and sticks tapping from the cabins all night. Us young ones running in circles before we finally fell sound asleep in somebody's lap. I hoped it'd be just like that.

Then John told us more about his farm. I didn't believe that either until he brought us yellow summer squash and purple onions from his own garden. Levi stared at such colourful vegetables growing in a country we'd been told was so cold. Made me worry he wasn't planning on eating them that night, just admiring them.

"Yessir, gonna buy us our own place someday like John," Levi said to the sky as we lay down in the dark that very night, squash, onion and bean stew filling our bellies.

Soon after that, we got to see John Bright's farm. It was up in the north part of Little Africa, past the railroad tracks. An acre of vegetables. Some hay. Two cows and a shed full of laying hens. A small farmhouse with grandbabies and young children on the porch. They all tumbled out when they spotted us. The young ones ran around us in circles, tugging each other's dresses and sleeves, playing tag like Master's grandchildren back home. They yanked on me to join their game. Like little chicks, they scattered in all directions. Such giggles clucked out of them all. They had all been born free. Though some of their mothers had been slaves, their fathers were born here in Canada.

"They never knew slavery," gasped Levi. "Imagine that! And

livin' with their whole family, ma and pa and grandparents too."

I let them yank me like some toy all over that field, running after them, plopping down beside them. I am sure I laughed too. But my laughter was no match for theirs — bright bells ringing loud and clear across the flat field.

I was right different from them. Beside them, I felt like a lone rooster, stiff and watchful. A dark web dropped over me like some spider spinning the names of Ma, Pa and Grandpa. I wanted to disappear at times. Or sun myself on some rock like a garter snake. Every chance I got, I slipped deep into the woods along the trails they say the natives once cleared, where such tall oaks grew, no light shone through. Thick and wide these ancient trees were. Wider than ten Levis standing side by side, they rooted to the ground with all their might.

The trees began to teach me. They stood so silent, taking in the sun or rain or wind. They just keep on. Standing over me like Grandpa once did, looking down, seeing everything up ahead that I couldn't see yet. Besides, there was nobody I could speak to. Levi was too busy being Levi to give a look my way anymore.

* * *

Then Levi remembered his promise to Grandpa and reminded me that I must go to Sunday School soon. I fought against him.

"I'm not ready for school yet," I told him. "Got things to learn about loggin'. Let me help you instead."

He grinned as he sliced his double-bitted axe clean through a log. "Got ants itchin' your pants? C'mon, I'll teach you how to slice clean through fresh wood with just a few blows."

Though I'd watched him and the others use that axe, I never imagined I could try.

"Swing straight down and it'll cut clean," Levi said. "Don't let it catch the wind or it might slip and slice your foot instead."

Blow after blow, he struck the log. Split pieces of wood shot here and there.

"Look here — " Levi pointed to a tough knot in the log. "Hard to cut through that. So it's best to whack it into pieces first."

This time, Levi turned the axe around so the opposite blade hit the knot, clearing it of the rough wood. He swung the axe again and it cut through smooth. The cutting blade was so sharp, it could split one of Levi's hairs. The other blade was dull and had a blunt end. Such a wonder this tool was. You could do the work in half the time.

Finally it was my turn. The axe was heavier than a single blade. I set a wedge into a crack in the log and heaved the axe down. The axe whizzed by, slicing through the air. It chipped away inch by inch and after many minutes, finally cracked the log open. In an hour, the two of us had stacked a big pile of split cordwood. My whole chest swelled like a robin's breast and my arms throbbed. "Growin' my own muscles," I bragged to Levi.

He joked back. "Time you got started growin' 'em. Been too scrawny."

Levi was all smiles. He seemed to enjoy teaching me what he knew. But I couldn't fool him. The next Sunday came along. Everything slowed down that day and I wanted to too. Church services bright and early for everyone and then the whole day free. But Levi insisted I stay behind for Sunday School.

Not many showed up at Sunday School, held upstairs in the hot rafters of the church. A few children, boys and girls so young that when they sat down, their feet didn't touch the floor. Some older men too. Soon their heads fell onto their chests and you could hear snoring. The room was bare except for our hard benches. A white woman, the preacher's wife, appeared. Plain and pale, in a long dress with a high collar. Her hair was tucked beneath her bonnet so you could not guess its colour. At church, I had seen her golden-headed children. "Flaxen-haired," one man said, describing their strange hair that shone like flax in the sun.

The woman stood with an open Bible and said words aloud to us. We repeated them back to her. But then the afternoon grew so hot that my eyes began to close too. I woke up and heard the children droning on and on about "wil-der-ness." Soon I nodded again. After a few Sundays, as we repeated the same words over and over, I finally guessed she was telling us a story I knew from back home. How people were cast out of their own land and travelled through the wilderness, a desert with no food or water. Until they walked into a new land — Canaan. That word I knew.

Now and again, the preacher's wife called upon someone who had lived in Little Africa a good while. They rose up and stood by her side, saying the words aloud as she pointed to each one in her Bible. Their words sounded hard and odd, like they didn't fit inside their mouths. Not like the preacher's wife, whose voice was light as music. They were reading, I supposed.

Mostly I held on to the rough underside of the log bench with both hands to stop myself from walking out into the sunlight. Daydreamed through the talk about sums. Or peeled off slivers of bark to pass the time until she let us out. Outside, I could be sitting by the riverbank to watch for a sign of

Grandpa. For he was still living in the wilderness while all these folks were busy reading Scripture.

I made all kinds of excuses not to go to Sunday School, but Levi paid me no mind.

"It's hotter up there than a bonfire. My shirt is soaked with sweat," I complained to him. "And besides, I'm not learnin'."

"You sure you don't read and do such things?" His eyes narrowed. "I thought those were the things they did in school."

"Ye–es," I told him. "But it's always Scripture readings. No other books except the big black one the preacher woman holds."

"Never mind that. She's an a-bo-li-tion-ist. All she wants is for us to better ourselves. How many folks around would do that?" Levi asked. "You are stayin' on."

If truth be told, I didn't know how many more Bible stories I could pretend I was reading.

Chapter 12
THE OTHER SIDE

July to August 1857

"STOP THINKIN'! START WORKIN'!"

That was the advice Levi always gave me when he saw me too quiet. Sometimes he'd catch me all by myself sitting on a log in the woods. Bet he thought I was daydreaming. But I wasn't. Just resting deep inside myself.

"Hard work knocks all the worries out of your head," Cato said as he axed into a tree.

The two of them were never still, always moving, always planning. They even competed to see who could save the most money. Soon Cato was working late into the bright summer evenings alongside Levi. The only time they rested was while I was warming the schoolhouse bench Sunday afternoons.

Folks stopped buying so much firewood. The July days got hotter and hotter. Mosquitoes landed day and night. My neck was itchy with bites and scratchings. Now and then some servants came by for wood to burn in kitchen cooking stoves. So mostly I kicked up dust or flung tree branches sky high between small chores.

"Stop that, Solomon. We got other fish to fry," John Bright said.

Meaning he was sending me up to Miller's Shipyard way north and east, right on the water, where they say you can see clear across to the shore of the United States, like you could touch it. I popped up and began running behind John Bright and the gang headed there with tall oxen dragging whole logs behind them.

"Gonna raft these logs and float 'em cross the Niagara River," Abram in the rear of the workers told me. "They're goin' to Tonawanda in New York, to be shipped across the country for buildin' ships and railroad ties."

I looked at the heavy logs bouncing on the ground as we wound through the clearings across the mile or so to Miller's Creek. Once those trees had a home deep in the ground. Now we were setting them free on the water. I couldn't wait to see it. Along the way we passed over the railroad line that cut right across our path. I set my feet flat on top of it. At last, I was standing on the railroad tracks.

John pointed. "These railroad ties were cut right here by our hands. These logs go everywhere."

In the moment he said that, I was sure I felt shaking beneath my feet. Crouching low, I set my ear down close to the rails. They were singing the way John said they might if a train was coming. Screeching in a high-pitched voice. Humming along the iron rails. Then the rails screamed.

Up I jumped as John shouted, "Here it comes! Watch out!"

Smoke puffed our way like dark clouds, so thick you couldn't see behind them. But you heard the roar and the whizzing as the shining railcar shot nearer and nearer, making us step back. I'd never been so close to one before, blasted by the wind of its passing. Even the cheeks of my face got flattened by the speed. It seemed so hungry, gulping down cords of Little Africa's wood into its fire-belly, greedy for more. This train was a live beast growling across the heart of Little Africa.

What would it pass on its journey and who was aboard? I kicked off and scurried after it, trying to chase it down. My heart pumped and my chest heaved and the men roared, their shouts and laughter ringing in the air. The breeze behind the train cooled me. I kept on running. Finally the train disappeared around a bend but it whistled back to me. Heartbeats pumped all over — in my throat, my calves, and in my feet. I glowed, inches taller. I skipped back to the men and we trudged slow again, behind the oxen.

By the river we came to a full stop. I strayed away from the men carting logs to the dock. Most were busy tying all the logs together with tight rope knots and setting them down into the water to float across. Several white men jumped right on top the logs and sailed along with them across the river, guiding the whole bunch of them to the opposite shore. The men stretched one way and then the other, balancing themselves with long poles. Some logs drifted away or tossed in the current, threatening to head downstream, until the men flung their poles wide and far out to steer them straight across the river again.

I looked over at Buffalo, wishing I was riding those logs across with the men. And I remembered too much, just like Levi warned.

Over there on the other side, a little farther upstream, was where we ran like rabbits in the dark in June, where we hid along the riverbank, where we left Grandpa behind. That blasted quick river still roared between, cutting us in half.

No word of him. Two of us free. One of us still in hiding.

Does he feel the sunshine on his grey head today? I wondered. Maybe he's seen this river up close and looked to the free shore and wished to come over, quick as he could. Why doesn't he? Does he know how close we are to him? Every night, I'd been calling to him and listening in the dark for his voice — something I told no one. I never heard his voice again after that first time.

Nearby, I saw John pause in his work. "How long do you think someone needs to heal a bad ankle?" I asked him.

"Depends how bad. Twisted or broken?"

"Broken."

"Broke all the way through or just a splinter? How old is this person? The old take longer to heal."

"He's my grandpa. And he's over there." I pointed.

"Your grandpa? Best not expect him for months. Most likely, he'll come over before winter sets in."

Two whole months had passed by already. Each day seemed to stretch out long as a year. I couldn't wait and wait anymore. When John said that, I felt like some boat that had been sailing fine in the wind until that moment had just sunk all the way to the bottom of the Niagara River. For the rest of that day, I was quiet. Though the men were singing and teasing one another, and their laughter rang all through the trees, the day was done. So were my questions.

The loggers talked about all their plans. Some argued about what to do and where to go in the huge land called Canada. I didn't want to listen. I wanted to set down here and wait. But they were walking back and I had to go with them.

"To be truly safe, you might want to go inland," Abram began. "I hear there's farmin' and cheap land in Buxton and in Dawn, way across this land. No one will find you there."

Another man complained. "That's too far to go. A month's journey by foot. There are cities close by where we'd be welcome — St. Catharines, Hamilton."

"In big cities, we can make better wages. More jobs too," said Henry.

John interrupted them. "What better place is there than Little Africa? We can be outside all day, breathing the fresh air."

"I lived through one Canadian winter workin' outdoors. That's enough for me," said Abram. "This place empties out then. I can get work on the rails. Or be a waiter at the city by the Falls come spring. It's full of tourists over there."

"Where do you think you'll head, then?"

"Maybe I'll make it all the way to Toronto. Plenty of us in the neighbourhood of St. John's Ward. We can own houses, grow gardens and there's lots of work."

"Besides, John, what's gonna happen when all these trees are cut down?" asked Abram. "Almost half the forest is gone now. Good for plantin' crops after that, not growin' trees."

"Well, I'm already farmin'," John answered. "It'll make money too, some day."

Little Africa was my home now. Although I did not want to wait one more day for Grandpa, I had to. When he came, he'd decide where we were going. Or maybe he'd like to set down right here.

* * *

Finally the day everyone talked about was here: Emancipation Day, August 1! Whenever men spoke about it, their eyes gleamed from laughing or crying, I did not know which.

John Bright announced to all the workers, "This is the day Britain set all its slaves free in 1834. Queen Victoria ended slavery for all her subjects. God save the Queen!"

John Bright took the lead in the parade that wound through the clearings of Little Africa all the way down to the Niagara River. He'd been a drummer boy, as young as me, in the battle of Lundy's Lane back in the War of 1812. Lied about his age back then, he said, just so he could join up with the British troops. He had saved those same drums that once made troops march into fighting. He was banging right hard on them now to make all the living jump through the streets.

At the river the parade stopped. John Bright climbed on top a stump where all the crowd could see him

"After you fight for a land, it owns you," he said to all those gathered there. "So I stayed here in Fort Erie and never left. This is my home. I own some of it now. And my whole family is livin' here on the Queen's free soil."

Everyone cheered. A handful of white folks came by to watch. I think I spotted Missus Forsyth among them. The Kival brothers, who leased the land for the logging operation, joined us with some church families. They cheered along with us. Then the Mission woman recited the Anti-Slavery Alphabet in a loud voice. Some folk set hankies to their eyes upon hearing it. I joined in the only part I knew:

U is for Upper Canada
where the poor slave has found
rest after all his wanderings,
for it is British ground!

There were lots of names they called this land. Canaan. Promised Land. Upper Canada, named that way because this country sat on top the St. Lawrence River. Or Canada West like Queen Victoria called it. To me, it was Canada, my home.

After the parade and speeches, there was dancing in the village clearing until late that night. It reminded me of back home and how we celebrated come corn shucking time. Grannie making sure I was scrubbed. Everybody singing and laughing. And the time my friend Augustus, Job's son, yanked me to do a crazy dance for a contest — cuttin' the pigeon wings, it was called. We flapped our legs and arms and bobbed our necks way out long like a pigeon. Grandpa's face so lit up as he watched me.

Now, in Little Africa, I sat on the edge of a circle around the dancers and just watched. Some men swinging their ladies in the air. Gingham skirts swirling. Laughter and loud voices. John's grandchildren high jumping, each one trying to leap higher. Clapping to the beat. Grown men dancing by themselves like fools. Levi was one of them. He kicked up dust with his leather boots and shouted something about freedom and queens.

I could not budge my feet to join in. Nobody I loved was here. Instead I sat still as a tree and watched other folks spinning free without me. I could tell no one that half of me lived on the other side, still in hiding.

Chapter 13
YANKED UP BY THE ROOTS

September 1857

DIDN'T KNOW WHETHER HE WAS TEASING or not, but one September day Levi passed by and stared at me. "Gettin' tall, Solomon. Freedom is growin' and eatin' enough every single day."

I sure could cart a heap more logs in my arms than I did when I first came across. Took me no time at all now to build up a high woodpile, all the ends lined up neat and straight, ready for selling once the cold set in next month. An axe hung on my belt every day like a trusted friend.

It was summer's end and still hot, but way different from Georgia heat. Southern heat gets inside you and never lets up. In your armpits, down your back and between your toes is a sweat bath. Even the shade is dripping hot down South with summer's breath blowing through like a forest fire. Summers here were hot too. Except when you headed into shade on the north side of a tree. Such a breeze gets trapped there. If you sat real still, you could feel dampness rise from the earth and climb your bare legs, sending cool shivers right up to your scalp.

Everything was working fine until the morning John Bright's boots stood by our tent as we awoke. He'd been waiting on us in the half-dark.

"Men passed through yesterday," he said in a low voice. "Searchin' for a tall man named Levi in the company of a boy and an old man."

75

Levi's whole body stilled. "What did they look like?"

"Two lean men. White. All in leather. Lined faces. I told them you were never here."

"The drivers from when we crossed!" Levi gasped. "They followed us."

"Don't worry. You can stay on here. The law in Canada West says no slavecatcher can bring you back over to the United States," John told us. "Not unless you committed a terrible crime. Then you must be returned."

Levi sighed. "I'm in big trouble if they find me."

"You did somethin' wrong? When? How old are you anyway?"

I never thought about how old Levi might be. Figured he was a grown-up. But he hadn't jumped the broom yet and taken a wife.

"Nineteen. I sure took my chances." Levi swallowed hard. "But I guess it was crime enough for Master to send slavecatchers after me and bang those posters up. That's why I ran, though it was still winter. Someone overheard Master settin' a trap for me that very night, so I had to go."

John Bright sighed. "Then I can't keep you safe. They may try to take you back and put you on trial. They'll track you down. You got to clear out of here and look after the boy. Can't leave him behind."

"Both of us got to go?" I asked. "What if Grandpa Jacob shows up at Bertie Hall? He might need help. Or come lookin' for us. And he won't find us here."

"Don't worry, Solomon. I'll send word there today to check if anyone came through. But no matter what news you hear, you both must leave tonight. Not safe to stay here. Those drivers will be snoopin' again real soon. I'll find you a way out."

I glared at the two men. Didn't they know I had to wait here for Grandpa? If I left, no one would keep watch for him. Three whole months had passed by. Surely he'd come across any moment now. I *had* to stay here.

Levi turned away from my stare. Though I felt like pounding on his chest, it would do no good to plead with him. John Bright didn't budge though. His face grew so sorrowful as he watched me. He was a grandpa too. Surely he'd remember to look out for mine and keep his promise.

He set his hand on my shoulder. "We got to keep you safe, son. When you're all settled, let me know where you are at and I'll be sure to tell Grandpa Jacob."

Levi stood up then and headed to the woods with his axe and saw. "Double time," he yelled back to John Bright. "Today I'm choppin' two trees for every one I used to bring down. Double the pay today."

John hollered back. "All right. Sure am sad you're leavin'. Hate to lose one of my best loggers."

Levi spent the day smashing down trees while I paced in front of our tent. Maybe, I thought, Grandpa had already come over and was resting at Bertie Hall without our knowing. He'd get word of our leave-taking in time to come with us; he'd be all healed up too. I'd better get ready for him.

I ran straight to the place where I'd been storing my coins. Dug them up with my bare hands and filled my pockets with their shine. Ran all the way to Charley. He'd been keeping a pair of fine boots for me. Each week I gave him some of the coins I earned as tips. Now I spilled the rest into his wide open hands. There was enough to buy those boots now.

"You sure they're your grandpa's size?" Charley shook his head and grinned.

"His feet are twice as long as mine and wide as my thigh," I told him. "These will fit."

The boots were black and high to the ankle, just the kind to hold Grandpa's thin legs up. But I didn't tell Charley why I needed them this very moment.

At dusk Levi returned, sweat-drenched and frowning. He looked at my belongings strewn everywhere like usual, not tied up to travel like his.

"Pack up. I hope you didn't say a word to anyone about us leavin'."

"No. But aren't we safe here like all the others?"

"We've been safe here all these months, and now this. Can't stop slavecatchers from comin' in here and can't stop anyone from talkin' to 'em. Whether I'm guilty of something or the slavecatchers just think I am, we got to leave."

"But, Levi . . . We planned to stay and wait on Grandpa Jacob. It's almost fall. John said he'd cross before winter. That's real soon. We *got* to wait."

Levi shook his head. "We must go *now*. Little Africa has been good to us both. But if those men catch sight of us, they'll know our faces. Can't stay here."

"Grandpa–"

Levi sighed. "Bertie Hall has seen no sign of him yet, John says. He'll tell no one but Jacob where we're headed. You have his promise. Get your things. A wagon with a load of lumber is headed west and we'll be boardin' it."

I'd been growing roots like some plant in Little Africa. But with those few words Levi yanked me up. He wasn't that much older than me, after all. He was not my elder. Why should I listen to him? He was bent on tugging me across free land like he once shouldered me to the Niagara River across the borderland. Back then, I'd fought him with my whole body, kicking. Now, even with all my new muscles, I didn't have a breath of strength to fight him.

If Grandpa ever got here, there'd be no sign of us. All I had of him was the boots slung over my shoulder.

Chapter 14
TO PORT DOVER

SCIPIO, AN OLD MAN, DROVE US AWAY from Fort Erie along the Talbot Trail. A bumpy road, rutted and muddy. Made me dizzy from the see-saw way we rode over it.

"This wood's gonna be made into furniture at Port Dover," he told us. "Be many days before we get there. You'll get a chance to see the land. Tho' when most folks go west, they never come back to Fort Erie. I always wonder about that. Are they safe or not? Do they settle down someplace better?"

I buried myself like a mouse between the straw and hickory wood in the back of Scipio's wagon. At our backs, the train whistled on its way home to Fort Erie, low, like it was saying goodbye. It would never take me anywhere now. The best way to get through this was to lay flat down and sleep deep, I told myself. But that wasn't easy. Sometimes the wagon hit a log and we'd go flying up high and land back down hard. Levi sat straight up, looking ahead. Whatever he was thinking, he told me nothing.

Of course I couldn't stop thinking either. The moment my eyes popped open, I shut them tight again. *How could Grandpa follow us across Canada now?* I wanted to fling myself clear out of that wagon and run the trail back. But I knew they wouldn't let me do such a thing. So I gritted my teeth tight and refused to speak. Even when Levi asked about the extra pair of boots I carried, I never answered. Just let silence brew between us, thick and dark as thunder clouds.

Each night we stopped to make a fire, cook some cornmeal mush and sleep outside.

"Sure is somethin' to sleep on British ground," Scipio sighed one night as we lay down.

"Is there any danger here from slavecatchers?" Levi asked him.

We had not breathed a word to our driver about why we left Fort Erie at night and neither had John Bright. And Scipio never asked about any trouble we'd had before we came away.

"If they catch hold of you and try to bring you back," he answered, "someone's gonna stop 'em. It's against the law to do that here. But some sneak in the dark and grab ex-slaves. Nobody's gonna save you then. Best to go inland, I hear, farther away from the States and slavecatchers too."

That night, Levi and I both slept inside the back of the wagon. He and I took turns listening in the dark, both of us worrying if we should have come this way.

After five days of travel, Levi unloaded the wood near Port Dover and we said goodbye to Scipio. At last I jumped onto solid ground. I wanted to run all over it, and feel it underneath my feet again, solid and hard and free like I thought Canada was, and leave that wagon behind. We planned on following the pathways along the lake and heading southwest, like Scipio told us.

Houses appeared along the path. Some clustered side by side. Some set alone with wide fields all around them. One old white woman standing on her porch, sweeping, as we passed by. She was lean up and down, faded. Even her apron was yellowed. As soon as she caught sight of us on the road, her broom stalled in mid-air and she followed us with just her eyes. Even after we'd gone a distance, when I looked back, still she stood motionless and silent, her narrowed eyes upon us. Back home, white folks often passed us by without seeming to even notice us. Like we were shadow people. Only those who owned us watched us like that lone white woman. What did she see when she looked at us — our raggedy work clothes, our big boots pounding, our skin shiny with sweat? Whatever it was, she did not like it. A great confusion set upon me. This country had called us to come over, but not all folks seemed to agree about it.

The blue of the lake soon came into view, and miles of sand. So cooling to look at it. A boatman hauled in his boat there. Levi got busy talking to him, since he looked like he was from back home.

"Afternoon! The boy and I are looking for a place to settle. What kind of work is there around these parts?"

"Fishin' mostly. Folks know where to find me — name's Owen — if they want fresh fish. Got regular customers in town I deliver to. Use my boat for haulin' goods down the lake too."

Levi asked. "You make a good livin' at it?"

"Enough to get by. We have more than we ever dreamed of back on the plantation. Pay a little to the landowner to live here. Keep busy all year long. Ice-fish in winter when the lake freezes over. Heat ourselves burnin' driftwood."

"You know of any jobs around here that pay a dollar for the day?"

Owen raised his eyebrows. "That kind of pay may be in the big towns, I suppose. But it's sure not around here. Why don't you join me for a couple of days and see how you like fishin'?"

Just then two boys rushed up to me. One older than me and one so young he wasn't talking yet. Both had big smiles bursting like sunflowers.

"You comin' through for the first time?" the bigger boy asked. His eyes were full of sparkles. Right away he reached out to shake my hand hard. "Don't worry. They can't come catch you. They are way over there. We been safe here two years."

He pointed across the wide sparkling lake. "Can't even see it, can you? It's gone and done with, my pa says. We never go to bed hungry. Or fear some master."

He swept his arms all around, toward the lake in front of him and the woods in back. "All we need is here. Fish. Pheasants. Deer. Duck. Geese. Berries — "

The younger boy yanked on the other's arm. He was holding a metal pail.

"All right, Abel. We'll go now." The boy smiled. "I'm Franklin and Abel's my brother. He wants to go berry pickin'. Wanna come with us?"

We joined hands with Abel and ran toward the woods. Levi and Owen waved us off. In and out of the bushes, down worn paths, we walked as Abel skipped behind us.

"Abel doesn't remember it," said Franklin. "He was born here. Not like me. I'm thirteen and I remember. Mostly at night. That's when the nightmares come."

I was like a dry rag soaking in his words. Words seemed easy for him, like soft butter spread on bread. I listened to Franklin say what I could not. Nightmares had come to me too . . . *Awakening in a sweat, heart pounding . . . Blood dripping into my hands as I reached out for Pa . . . Running . . . Someone on our trail . . . Grandpa Jacob's hand saluting air . . . His face turned away . . . If only Grandpa's hand had grabbed me back to stay with him instead . . .* These were secrets I could tell no one.

In the woods, a berry patch sat bright in a sunny spot. I

stopped thinking and just stared. Loads of prickly bushes with plump blackberries hung on the ends of branches.

"One for the pail. One for our mouth. That's our rule." Franklin began picking. I popped a berry big as my thumb into my mouth. Tart and sweet. Crunchy.

"Mmmm!" I said.

"M . . . mm . . . mmm!" echoed Abel.

We laughed, pinging berries into the pail and filling our bellies too. Round and round the bushes we circled. These berries were free for the asking. Only the birds and us knew about them. And we had beat the birds that morning.

Our pail was soon full so we ran off. Back at the river, the boys' family lived in a small tin shack set back from the beach in the shady woods. There was a fire pit outside and clothes flapping on a line. We set out the berries to dry in the sun on top a log. Levi and Owen were busy sawing wood. It was so hot that afternoon with the sun beating down and no clouds. Our shirts stuck to our backs.

"Race you to the water!" Franklin yelled.

The three of us ran to the water. Waves pushed into shore and then tugged away over and over like deep, long breaths. Franklin and Abel didn't stop at the edge but splashed into the lake, diving under and bobbing up. You could hear them screaming and laughing all down the shoreline. Franklin kept calling me to join them.

The lake was wide, without an ending or a beginning. Twenty or so miles across, Franklin had said. It stretched in all directions. Bet it had no bottom. The Niagara River had been cold and wild, full of currents moving so swift that my feet never touched down. I dared not go in this water now.

"Come on in!" Franklin kept calling.

Abel waved. He was far out but even he was still standing. I could see his knees.

"Sandbars!" Franklin shouted. "We're not over our heads yet."

They both seemed to be standing up. So I dipped my toes in. The water was so warm, melting warm. I could see minnows, tiny as my fingernails, darting around my toes. I stepped in. Abel splashed close by and grabbed my legs and we both fell into the water.

The three of us had a splashing fight. Laughing and screaming while we threw handfuls of lake water and kept falling down. When we finally came out, near dusk, we were soaked.

Franklin ran off for fishing poles and we stuck them in and waited. Cool at last. I yawned some, ready to fall asleep, when we saw rippling in the waves — something yellow with black stripes.

"Perch are runnin'!" Franklin whispered.

When my pole yanked hard, I pulled back. The line shook with a fish on the end, half an arm's length. After we pulled in five fish, Franklin ran over to the fire pit and his ma cooked them so fast, we all plopped right on the sand to eat.

Hot fried perch, dipped in flour and garlic. Sweet and soft. Flaky. Hardly chewed it at all. It slid down salty and greasy and hit my stomach sizzling. Followed by crunchy corn pones from a black skillet, like back home. Hot herb tea. Licked my fingers and made sure I got every crumb. Never felt so hungry.

All you can do after a dinner like that is lay back. And so we did. Franklin's ma brought out some canvas and we stretched out on the shore, wiggling our bare toes deeper and deeper down into the cool sand. Above us, the stars lined up. It was very dark when we were still awake. That's when the owls started up, hooting from the woods, "Whoo! Whoo! Whoo!" We answered their every hoot, calling out after they had their say first. Back and forth we spoke to them while we swatted the mosquitoes buzzing in our ears. Levi was snoring by then. Abel was curled up on Franklin's chest. We pulled our blankets up to our chins and shut our eyes. Even the air smelled so damp and close, it felt like home.

For the first time in my life, I wanted something I could never even imagine before: to stay right here with Franklin and Abel, my new friends. This was Canaan for now.

Chapter 15
ACROSS CANADA WEST

LONG DAYS PASSED IN PORT DOVER, days of running hard, playing most of the day and sleeping deep. Us kids fished from shore every day while the men floated in Owen's boat. Though Owen trained us all how to bait our hooks and when to dunk them, everyone landed perch except Levi.

He drifted to shore one evening, stepping out of the boat, scowling. "Too much sittin'. Makes me restless. This is not for me."

Owen shrugged. "What work do you like to do?"

"Movin' and sweatin'. Haulin' and liftin'. That makes me feel strong, like I'm standin' on top of the world."

Owen laughed. "You sure are a good deal younger than me! I'm suited to sittin' and waitin' for a fish to grab my bait."

The next day after breakfast, I knew what Levi would say. My stomach told me; it was so jumpy, I hardly ate a bite.

"I don't mind workin' hard but I want to farm my own land, like John Bright," Levi announced. "Got to make money every single day. So we have to move on."

Franklin's quick and easy smile vanished.

"Can't we stay a while?" I begged Levi. "Lots to do here and food everywhere. Franklin and I could — "

"Remember what we promised your grandpa?" Levi shot back. "There's no school in Port Dover. Not enough children around for a school, Owen says. So we gotta move west. Be safer there anyhow, Solomon. Maybe we could join a settlement."

My stomach rose up to my throat.

Owen nodded. "In this country, you have a say when you vote. Got to live here three years to get it. You become a British subject then. When you vote, you can ask for a school and get it. Around here, we live day to day. Not enough coloured families around to make a difference yet. Don't have much money. Or schoolin'. But my boys are happy. So we are stayin'."

Franklin pumped my hand hard again, like he did when we met. But this time, it was slow and sad. "Wish you could stay here with us," he said. "But you got to find the best place for yourselves."

"This *was* the best place," I told him.

* * *

Those were the last words I spoke for a long while. Levi was always the one to decide; he thought he was the boss in charge of me. Can't even tell you about the rest of the roaming we did. Like vagabonds, we lit out to the west. I shut my ears to all Levi's plans about farming and hurrying before frost hit to get settled and his naming all the vegetables he was gonna plant. Like tobacco, collards, corn and red oak lettuce. Didn't want to hear about it.

I couldn't keep the names of new places straight. They all passed by like a dream. Farmlands and woods. Afternoons when the sun blazed so hot we peeled off our shirts to cover our heads. Once, we passed by a group of white children splashing themselves by their well. Their pa motioned us to come by. He surprised us by passing us a bucket we could use to haul up ice water from deep in that well. We drenched ourselves down first, shivering cool, then the young ones who begged over and over for a splashing of that cold water. We laughed and thanked them before walking on. Views of Lake Erie and the quick dunks we took. The soles of my used boots flapping open now. The raggedy folks we met, headed to Wilberforce or Toronto. Some to Owen Sound. Some, like us, not knowing where to go.

"Schoolin'?" one traveller questioned us. "Best not to go Windsor way. Tho' laws are changin', I heard there was trouble in Sandwich over a school."

"You mean they don't have any?"

"They got 'em but don't want to share 'em with us. When our children showed up, the white children all disappeared. Their families kept them home. So the town put up a notice on the door: *Select School*. Meaning that only whites were invited in."

Levi's eyes narrowed. "Folks won't let us have good schoolin' after all we been through to get here?"

"You might find it different elsewhere. If I were you, I'd go to bigger towns like Chatham, Hamilton or Toronto. Those places have many schools. Some allow our kids to attend. Chatham's not far from there. Just head inland as soon as you pass the docks at Port Stanley."

We passed by farms haying their last crop of the season. Levi called out to the farmers on their horses, "Got any work? We work for food and cash. No handouts. Got a farm to buy."

Haying for days until my back couldn't pull itself up straight. Knocking down dried cornstalks until my fingers bled, and still splitting them into piles.

Beans every night. I do remember that. Brown ones and pink ones and freckled ones. Never soaked long enough and never enough time to cook them down, they pinged in our bellies all night and the next day too. We never stopped long enough in one place to catch a rabbit, though Levi did stone a bird down now and then. I daydreamed about meat. Dripping with grease, straight from the fire, pretend rabbit legs melted in my mouth.

Overnight, the trees began to burn into orange and red and gold. At first I thought I was imagining it. Just a blush at first, gentle colours, and then that red that looked like the trees were flaming. It was shocking to see the world blazing bright with colour, all the green dying, while the days turned shorter and cooler. Walking on and on.

* * *

One cool night, we slept by the water and awoke to great mists everywhere. From the lake rose clanging and voices. Something dark came into view. A huge ship churned across the lake at full speed, coming straight at us. When it neared the shore it stopped. We were close enough to see white folks standing on deck and hear their shouts. Soon ropes swung out and Levi and I crouched behind boulders to watch. We couldn't believe our eyes. A plank was thrown down from the ship. A group of raggedy families scurried down it onto a small boat — men, women carrying babies, and some children. Shouts of "Goodbye!" and "Good luck!" from on board and passengers waving as the small boat landed on shore and the people stepped out and thanked the oarsmen.

"You're in Port Stanley now," passengers called out to them from the ship. "Godspeed to freedom!"

We waited until the ship sailed off. Then we burst out from behind the rock to where the folks were laughing and hugging. Children ran in circles and chased one another. Such shiny eyes they all had.

An old man looked at us. "You two safe here?"

Levi nodded. "Welcome to Canada. You must be happy to come."

"Been a long journey. Most of us ran from Kentucky. Others joined us along the road. Abolitionists in Ohio led us all aboard this boat. Got a free ride with the captain. Said a hundred families have crossed over with him this year."

I gasped. Such a wide lake to cross and so many had sailed across so easily.

Another man joined us. "We're headed to the Dawn Settlement near Dresden. You know it?"

Levi shrugged. "We heard of it. But haven't been there yet."

"Due west inland, the abolitionist said, away from the lake. Follow a river to a main road, then cross the Thames River. Seven days walk, if we don't stop."

He looked at an old woman who had plopped down in the sand to rest.

"What's in Dresden?" I asked.

"Like I said. A settlement called Dawn. People farm it. Josiah Henson used to run it. He crossed over at Fort Erie."

"We crossed near Fort Erie too!" said Levi. "Worked in Little Africa."

"Who owns that? Coloured folks or whites?"

Levi paused. "Whites own it. But a man named John Bright runs it."

"Up in Dawn, folks have their own land and a school too. That's why we're headed there. Gonna work and save enough to get our own place in the settlement. Even got a letter from the abolitionists to introduce ourselves."

I poked Levi right in the ribs. "Why don't we go with 'em?"

Levi stepped back. "I sure am tired of roamin' for work before the season ends. But before we settle, I need to save enough to buy land and be able to build a cabin too. So I'm not ready to go there yet. Maybe we'll join you someday."

"Well, we wish you and the boy luck wherever you go." The man waved goodbye to us, then called to his friends, "C'mon everyone, let's head to Dawn."

Dawn. It sounded like a new beginning, another Canaan. The group rose up, gathering the children, and headed into the woods. I watched until their bodies grew smaller and smaller. Their back-home voices and shiny faces filled me up like I was in Little Africa again among so many friends. Between Levi and me, silence dropped down like a net again. He headed away from the lake too, travelling inland for the first time. He stepped with his eyes straight ahead and his arms swinging. I had no choice but to follow.

Maybe I was lost in my own thoughts, kicking up dust when it happened. Maybe I would have seen it first. Levi was just about to walk up the path to a farmer's house to ask for work when a white man yelled from his barn, his shotgun pointing straight at us, the trigger pulled back.

"Trespassers!" the man shouted. "Stay off my property or I'll set the law after you. We don't want your kind here. I only hire whites."

Hearts pumping, running hard down the road, we were like hopping rabbits. In the wide open field, our backs could be clearly seen. Never disappeared so quick. Levi pushed me right in front of him, startling me. He'd take the shot first, I realized afterward. We hid the whole day after that, deciding to tiptoe our way through that county. We sunk down in fields to sleep, the corn high and dry, the stalks rustling like a herd of grasshoppers in the wind. Up before dawn and moving on.

I jerked awake in a tobacco field in the middle of one night.

My clothes were drenched with sweat from some nightmare. In it, someone was aiming a gun at Grandpa, making him jump up and down. I was screaming to him to run away but he just hopped like a rabbit and didn't seem to hear me. Then I saw the man's face, the one with the gun. It was Master. He'd come after us. He demanded Grandpa tell him where Levi and me were at. "Don't tell him!" I shouted.

That's when I woke up with a pop. *Nobody can follow our trail right now,* I told myself. *Not even Grandpa. We don't know where we are goin' at all. We are lost.*

I didn't think freedom would be like this: sneaking around and doing whatever Levi said; not knowing who would welcome us and who would shoo us off; nowhere to belong to. I thought freedom would be a whole lot different. We could have settled easy with Franklin's family; we'd go fishing and berrying all day long. Grandpa Jacob sure would have liked it there, stepping down firm on the sand in his new boots.

Still his voice sometimes hummed in my head once I got so tired I couldn't think anymore. *Wait on me, Solomon,* I heard him say as we walked another mile long past dusk to nowhere in particular.

Chapter 16
THE SMELL OF CANADA WEST

October 1857

ONE SUNDAY AFTERNOON, as we walked on and on through the brush, we got a whiff of meat roasting. In every dream I'd ever had about Canada, there was meat cooking. No mistaking that smell — nothing in the world smelled as good as that. We were both starving. At a clearing, Levi stopped. There was a crossroads there with a store, church, farmhouse and a building made out of logs. We walked closer and peeked in the windows. It was empty inside except for the desks lined up in rows, too many to count. One big desk up in front. Books lying everywhere in piles.

Levi smiled. "It's a schoolhouse!"

Off a little ways was a general store. Boxes piled up in front. Smoke rose from out back where meat on a spit was roasting over a fire. We headed straight over.

Levi pointed. "What's the name of that school?"

"Bloomfield," said the shop owner. "This is Raleigh Township. Finally got a teacher for the year and this school's crowded."

"Is this school for white children only, or can Solomon here go too?"

The man's eyes narrowed. "Both. They figured a way for them both to learn. Saved the town a heap of money because they pay for just one teacher."

"Sounds fine to me," Levi said. "Any work around these parts?"

The man looked Levi up and down some minutes. I do admit there was a lot of him to see.

"You just passing through? We get plenty of drifters out of these woods. I give them a job and train them. Next thing I know, they're gone with no warning. And I've got no one to load supplies from the railroad or chop wood for winter."

"Well, sir, I can do most anythin'. I cut down trees all summer, near the Falls. I need regular work now that farm season's endin'."

"Tell you what. If you stay until spring, I'll raise your pay an extra twenty cents a day then. Start at fifty cents. You look like the man for the job. When can you start?"

Levi hesitated, enough to let me know he was thinking on it. He'd made much more in Little Africa.

"Tomorrow mornin'," decided Levi. "First, I'll bring the boy to school. Got to find us a place to stay tonight though."

Levi was settling down in this nowhere spot by a crossroads, just like that. None of it with my say. All because of a schoolhouse.

The man pointed. "There's a boarding house down that road a half mile. They'll take you in. But first, help yourself to some venison cooking out back. My missus will help you. See you here bright and early."

Levi grinned all that evening. He grinned at the shop owner and his kindly wife, at the taste of sweet smoky venison, at the boarding-house woman, when she said she had come from Georgia too, and when she said yes, she had room for us. I wasn't grinning at all and Levi didn't even notice. In the morning, I'd be going to a proper school. There were loads of books inside that log schoolhouse. If they had books, they had words.

Back on the plantation, old Grannie called words the Devil's scratchings. "Why else do you think they blacken a pretty white page so?" she hollered.

"But where do they come from?" I once asked her.

"From the fires of Hell!"

Master Tiller and his family set such store on reading and writing. They sat around with books and paper and ink pens most every night. Some books were so secret, I suppose, that they were locked behind glass. That's what Violet told me. But if we were caught anywhere near a book, there'd be ten lashings like the ones poor Violet got from the Mistress for opening up a book and peeking inside after she dusted it along with the furniture. She said she was so lost in its golden pictures, like she was stepping into another world, that she hardly felt those lashings.

"Such evil ones follow nothin' but evil!" Grannie fussed. "Bound to be spells in those words they look at. Why do you think we can't touch 'em? Don't go near books!"

Grannie got so worked up at such times, spit flew right out of her mouth. You'd better duck if you were near her at such a fussing. She'd sure get out her broom to swat Levi on the side of his head right then if she heard what he had in store for me. He'd said the word "school" one too many times that day.

How come every time Levi had a plan for me, I felt like running? So I beat it outside at dusk, kicking stones and stirring dust clouds along the road, wandering alone.

Something was brewing inside me and now it became clear what it was. All my life I'd spent most every second outdoors — Georgia or Canada, it didn't make a difference. Long before first light on the plantation, the drivers pointed us to the fields. That's where I spent most of my daylight hours. Even when the day's work was done, I wouldn't go inside our cabin. Too dark without windows. Full of shadows inside. I stayed outside with Grandpa, working our small garden patch until I couldn't see, then go out hunting possum after dinner.

Dusk was my favourite time, when the light fades and hides everything and no one can call you to work anymore. You can just do as you please then. Some nights back home, especially in summer, I'd stretch out flat on the ground and fall asleep watching the stars pop out and line up next to the other stars like family. On such clear nights, I never wanted to step a foot inside. I was part of the earth and sky, my grandpa taught me, a wild woods creature. If I see the sun shining, I have to be outside. That's why I could have settled easy on the shore of Lake Erie fishing with Franklin. Even in Little Africa, I'd been surrounded by trees and space and stars, just the way I liked it.

Sticking me in that schoolhouse with books was like sticking a wildcat in a cage.

Chapter 17
LIES IN BLACK AND WHITE

WE WERE THE FIRST ONES at Bloomfield School next morning. Before sun-up we sat ourselves down on the wooden fence to wait. Two boys showed up, then three young girls, all of them white, lining up at the front door. One of the boys carried kindling and cut wood in a bundle. Levi and I didn't move. Just watched and waited some more.

One mournful looking boy walked past. He took one look at us and then nodded his head to the side. "Over there. That's where *we* go."

He pointed to a lean-to at the far side of the schoolhouse. It had a small slanted roof with three walls, one of which was the outside wall of the schoolhouse. One whole side was open to the wind. Other children came along and joined that boy, none of them white. There were about nine in all. I stood up to join them, but Levi held me back.

"We're waitin' on the schoolmaster."

A white man appeared, tall as Levi and skinny as a broomstick. No fat anywhere except if you count the flapping underneath his chin. All in black he was dressed, in a suit shined by so many ironings you could see the sun on it. His black hair was parted in the middle, slicked flat with oil, and hung down past his collar.

"Schoolmaster Wellington is the name," the man announced in a loud voice as he approached, causing all the children to turn his way. "What can I do for you?"

He did not offer his hand to Levi as menfolk do, though Levi had taken off his cap to greet him and held out his own hand. Instead, the man handed the oldest white boy a key. The door opened and all the white children disappeared inside without a murmur. I could see the tall boy stoking a wood stove. Another boy opened a window. The children in the lean-to did not move. There wasn't even room for all of them to fit underneath the awning. Some stood in the tall weeds.

"This here is Solomon. I promised his family he'd be schooled. You have a place for him? He's been to a Sunday School and heard some words from the Bible before. Knows some numbers too. But he's sure not readin' or writin'."

Mister Wellington pointed to the lean-to. "Over there. I'll give you papers to bring home and sign so it's official he's going to school."

Levi stood full straight, so I knew we were in trouble. He dared ask a question. "Why can't he go inside?"

Outside, the boys made big eyes and one elbowed another.

"This is what the Township decided. Got forty whites, more than enough, filling this classroom. Overflow goes outside. They can learn just as well there if they listen."

Levi pointed to some empty desks inside.

"Consumption," the schoolmaster explained. "Sick children best stay home. Can't learn if their heads are dropping down."

The sun was full up by then. Levi had to go. He took the papers from the schoolmaster, put his cap on square, and turned to me. "You listen good, Solomon. Make your grandpa proud."

I didn't dare look at the schoolmaster. I looked at my beat-up boots and watched them head over to the lean-to. Such a silence everywhere. Through the open window, we could peek inside the schoolhouse. All eyes set on the schoolmaster. He drew up his chest like spring's first robin. The boys and girls inside and out took a deep breath and began: "Our Father who art in heaven, hallowed be thy name . . ."

The words were the same ones as I heard at the Sunday School and back home too. To me, this prayer was about someone asking his father to stay in his grace always. It was beautiful if it was true. But in this schoolmaster's mouth, it sounded like some speech Master Tiller made before all of us slaves lined up when somebody got into trouble, all the words big sounding, but with no meaning at all. The schoolmaster watched each child, noting which ones didn't keep up. I mumbled along. Some words came right up to my lips without my thinking them. They were from remembering, I suppose.

Then the class sang a sad hymn. It was followed by a Bible reading about wheat and chaff, the good part you keep and the bad you throw away. Everyone listened, still as hens on a nest of eggs. My eyes strayed over the children and schoolmaster in the classroom. I couldn't see any difference between the whites and us except they were inside and we were outside. Most of the whites were ratty tatty like me, with thinned-out clothes from too much wearing, and leggings too short from growing. There was one girl, though, in a fine blue dress that swished when she moved. It lay around her like a cloud as she sat.

"We may as well review the alphabet first," announced the schoolmaster after we sat down. "Maybe this time, someone will get the letters correct."

He turned to the blackboard. An elbow poked me in the ribs in the same moment and then something trickled down my collar. Felt like hard stones against my bare back. It made me wiggle. Mister Wellington turned around just as my mouth opened. I clamped it shut. That's because there, on the blackboard, were scratchings like the ones Grannie had warned me about. Schoolmaster Wellington took out a long cane and beat it against the blackboard with each sound.

"A," he announced.

"A!" answered the class.

"B," he said.

"B!" all answered.

We joined in under the lean-to, or at least pretended to. One boy beside me had his mouth open wide, but no sound came out. Another shouted. I dared not open my own mouth for fear of making the wrong sound. So I just listened to those around me. As a listener, I had always been safe before. It was never proper for me to speak out loud.

Then the schoolmaster ordered us to copy those letters down. A slate pencil and a small slate got passed to me. So many heads were in my way I could not study the blackboard. So I watched the others in the lean-to wiggle their fingers and I tried to make those same strange shapes too. In my hands, the pencil was fat. It made such awkward lines, all wobbly, and I had to press down hard to even see what I wrote. It looked nothing like the marks the schoolmaster wrote. Except they were white, just like his.

Then I remembered what Grannie said. If God meant for us to write, we'd be born with the know-how, she once told me. Like how she knew when babies were ready to come or which leaves to pack a wound with. Well, folks sure are not born knowing which mushroom is safest to eat. That's why one of Master's young sons died, from eating the poisoned ones out in the woods. You learned about it from someone. Same as birthing babies or picking herbs. Someone's got to teach you first.

Grannie had it backwards.

It never occurred to me before that Grannie could ever be wrong. Though we sometimes poked fun of her behind her back, deep down I always believed whatever she said. Maybe she blamed reading words for making Master mean. She thought him full of something powerful if he could own us slaves. He was likely born into meanness. There must be something mighty strong inside words, though, for white folk to set aside a whole building like Bloomfield School to study them.

And then a wondering filled me. Maybe Grannie had warned me against words because she feared what would happen to me if I dared try to read. Whippings or slicing off fingers were the punishments for such a thing on our plantation. I had no ma or pa to tell me what to do. Maybe she was just trying to protect me. Maybe she loved me after all, like I loved her.

So I tried to write too, not really knowing how. Writing letters seemed like drawing, the way I used to scratch pictures in the dry winter dirt with a stick. If you put enough things in the picture, it told a story. So maybe it was the same with letters. They sure seemed a mystery, strung up on the wall and on the blackboard, some almost twins like E and F, but not quite. Some odd like Z. None of them made any sense. I copied as many as I could, lowering my head the whole while, just like I was back on the plantation, working. Not up to me to question, only to do.

On the way home that first day, I dared speak to the boys from the lean-to. Which one had played the trick with the stones falling down my back, I did not know. They were all laughing and skipping along so I figured they'd be easy to talk to.

"How long are you held up in winter?" I asked them.

"What do you mean, 'held up'?"

"Well, when it snows, can you still breathe? And can you find your way out of your house or do you have to wait 'til spring?"

Each one looked at the other one. Then somebody broke out laughing and they all started hooting. One boy even rolled on the ground saying his belly hurt.

"Snow?" roared Elmer. "You got to shovel it first. Then you got no excuse but to go to school."

"Wish this boy was right — that it could snow so much, we could stay home all winter long!"

I clamped my mouth tight. There sure were some things best kept quiet, like most things I heard from house slaves and Grannie both. All those warnings from Violet about the wilderness that was Canada. Being in Master's big house so much, she liked to eavesdrop on Master's storytelling. He'd never been to Canada himself, most likely. But he swore that in Canada, wolves sneaked in bold as crows and stole children away to live with them in the wilderness. Or ate them up on the spot. And that so much snow covered the houses in Canadian winters, those inside couldn't breathe and soon died. Bet he told those lies in a loud voice so Violet would hear and spread the word to all us field hands so we dared not run there.

They were all dead wrong about Canada.

There's something worse than wolves and snowstorms and wilderness. It's school. Not one word would I tell Levi about how much I hated it.

Chapter 18
A FLOCK OF CROWS

November 1857

IT STAYED GREY FOR DAYS ON END. The skies darkened as I walked the half mile to school. It rained and it poured, filling my boots full up through all their holes. No shelter beneath that lean-to, either, for the biggest, strongest ones got the inner wall of the schoolhouse. Guess where I sat? Newcomer and scrawny, I was on the outside of the outside, in the wind. Even the girls got better. So skinny they could wiggle their way in, pressing close to the bigger boys where I would never go.

Nobody liked it crammed all together like fish in a pail. Wet clothes that didn't dry out the whole day long. The smell of damp wool everywhere. Shoving something awful to get close to the warm wall. The first one to complain at recess was Elmer. He was the biggest one.

"What we got to stay in school for? Better to be workin' for money like my cousin in Chatham. He loads ships on the Thames River there."

"Gettin' to be cold," said another. "By Christmas, we can stay home. My ma won't make me walk four miles to school then. I'll work inside with my pa buildin' furniture."

The rain made me yawn and wish for sleep. We spent whole afternoons copying words from *The Canada Spelling Book* onto our slates. Such squeaking from our slate pencils. If I could only head off for a walk, I could warm myself and wake up too. But I couldn't go anywhere. Mister Wellington

104

fixed us down like flies beneath a swatter with his hard stare.

At the boarding house, a bad mood had spread that month too, just like the November weather. I overheard Levi in the parlour one night, talking to the others who had come here along the underground road, men of all ages and colours.

"They are payin' us less, I tell you," he said. "White workers earn more here. And I get the heavier load too. Between room and board, I can't save much. In Little Africa I earned a silver dollar a day."

His voice was low nowadays. He wasn't grinning like a fool anymore. But he didn't let on anything when he was with me. And I held quiet about school. If Grandpa wanted me to be learning, I had no choice but to go. It seemed Levi and me made a silent promise never to speak about these things.

* * *

When recess came at school, all the children ran around and around the yard outside. White girls came close up and studied my face and asked me all kinds of questions about where I'd been and where I'd come from. Traveller, they called me. Eleven whole years I'd spent on one plantation and never stepped down the road. But I'd gone hundreds of miles to reach Bloomfield and every child seemed curious to hear how I'd done it.

"Sure not somethin' I'd do again," I told them right off.

Betsy lost her smile when I said that. She was the one with that blue dress, the prettiest girl I ever did see. So soft was that dress when it brushed up against me once, like feathers. She had such tall legs, none of the other girls could catch her. I pretended not to be able to either, though I easily could.

In the outside classroom, we had to stand for prayers and hymns and when called upon to answer a question. We squatted on our heels for our lessons. We could rise up and take a peek through the windows to see the blackboard though. Rest of the time we always had to have our slates on our laps with our slate pencils ready. No talking was allowed. Those were the schoolmaster's rules.

In the lean-to, we had our own rules. We whispered some. Plenty of kicking, jabbing in the ribs and yanking of shirt-sleeves. You couldn't let them know you were ticklish, other-wise they'd be poking you in the armpits forever. But we couldn't carry on too loud or Mister Wellington would hear us. Mostly we took to shoving when the ones inside were singing some hymn so loud, or when the schoolmaster was so busy, there was no chance of him hearing us.

But when Mister Wellington faced the class, we were still as peas in a pod. We never knew what mood he was in, or how peeved he might get if we didn't learn quick enough. So those in the lean-to didn't dare to answer a question. Or ever ask one. Besides, he always held that cane, flicking it against the floor to get our attention. Worst of all was if he caught you doing something you weren't supposed to do. Like doodling. Or shooting a dried pea. Such a fuss there'd be. All work ended and the schoolmaster would let go a sermon so long, even a preacher would have trouble keeping up with him. Whoever was caught would spend the rest of the day in the corner star-ing at the wall. Mister Wellington would walk them home to their door and tell their parents too.

Then came the day of my first spelling test.

Mister Wellington passed out pencils and exercise books to write in. "Put your name on the top. When I call out a word, spell it on one line. Then go to the next line when I say the next word. Let's begin."

Outside, nobody moved. Nobody wrote their name down

except Elmer, who lifted his book high to show all of us his scratchings. I remembered how Elmer had taught me my name. So I wrote it on top of my page.

"The first spelling word is *Matthew*. MATT-THEW," the schoolmaster announced.

My pencil stopped in mid-air. An awful chill tickled me, making me shiver. Heat waves rose up and down my body. My wool pants stuck to my legs, cold and wet. I held my breath to stop a sneezing fit.

"Next is LUKE. Do you understand what words I am dictating to you?"

Inside, a hand flew up. A boy rose to his feet. "Sir, you are reciting the names of the apostles."

"Indeed I am, boy. Well done. Let's continue."

Such a silence like a spell over the whole schoolhouse, inside and out, as the schoolmaster said the words and the children tried to set them down. If we could trap the words down on the paper, they'd be ours. Sneezes flew out of me instead. None of those words got written in my exercise book. Mine was blank except for *S*, which Elmer swore was my name written down.

That's what made all the trouble.

"Which one of you is *S*?" the schoolmaster demanded after lunch, an exercise book waving in his hand, marked with red.

Everyone underneath the awning leaned away from the window so just my fool head stuck up.

"Did no one teach you your rightful name, boy?"

I sprang to my feet. For the first time, he was speaking directly to me. I swallowed such a fat gobber, it popped my ears. "Sir, Mis-ter Well-ing-ton . . . it's . . . Sol-o-mon." I said. "Ah . . . AAH . . . CHOO!"

"I see you know how to divide into syllables," the schoolmaster announced to the laughter of the white students. "But no clue how to spell it. Can someone spell it for him?"

He made a lesson out of my name, calling on this one and that one, sounding it out and writing the letters on the blackboard. Seemed to take forever until they answered it right enough for him. Not one of the outside students raised their hands.

"The ending is spelled *m-o-n*, not *m-a-n*," he taught them.

When it was all done, he made me copy that name onto my slate. Later, he came by to check. I passed my slate to him through the open window.

"Press down harder. Keep your hand steady. These letters are shaky."

It was the first time I wrote a real word in my whole life. Should have made me jump with joy. But it did not. For a singsong kicked up in the lean-to as soon as he left. Like a chorus of frogs, my classmates chanted my name low and hissing: "Sol-o-mon! Sol-o-mon!"

How stupid that name sounded. Why did it have to have so many letters? By the end of the day, I wished I had any other name but that one.

That name followed me all down the road. Older boys and younger ones too, from both inside and outside the schoolhouse, hooted and hollered at me like a flock of crows as I made my way home. They even teased me about my ears sticking out, same as they did back on the plantation. One thing's sure: boys are boys no matter where they live.

I ran looking for Levi at the store. Just his presence alone made most boys swallow their laughs real quick. I wanted to scream out my ignorance of not knowing how to write my own name, of not even having a last name except for Master Tiller's name that I did not want at all, and would tell nobody. Every time I thought about the schoolhouse, my head hurt and I began to cough without stop. If only I could confess how hard learning was. If only someone could help me understand the secret of letters. Or just give a listen to me. Only with Grandpa had it been safe to tell all. When he was around, whatever was in my heart flew to him. At that moment, it felt like my voice, sore and hoarse, was locked up tight in a box with no key to open it.

I did not find Levi, even in the cellar of the store. He was off at the railroad, looking for better work. He would not want to hear my complaints anyway. I stayed down in the cellar long as I could, busting my fists into the wall and pretending they were the faces of Elmer and his friends. If they had known how to spell some, I wouldn't have looked so stupid. Elmer could have taught me better, and given me more than an *S*.

Then it came to me. Those boys had been there much longer than me, for months and months this school year. If they still couldn't even spell their own names, how did the schoolmaster expect *me* to? Maybe it was the schoolmaster who was wrong. Maybe it was *him* who didn't know how to teach boys and girls who had never been to school before.

For over a week afterwards, I stayed in bed at the boarding house, with fever and a barking cough that kept Levi and me up most of the night. Chills flashed through me like thunder and lightning, hot and cold at the same time. Nightmares rode past like an endless train. *Pa's face so squeezed in pain. His eyes flat without any shine, like he was dead. My hands drenched in blood. Somebody whisking me off and then Pa was no more.* When I could finally sit up, my legs felt as thin and quivery as chicken legs.

When I returned to the schoolhouse, I couldn't look at Mister Wellington and lift my head up anymore. It was him on one side and me on the other like he was talking at me through a fence. I closed my heart to him and all his teachings.

Chapter 19
ON THE OUTSIDE, LOOKING IN

Early December 1857

WE ALL LIKED TO MAKE FUN of the schoolmaster. Miles, one of the inside boys, gathered us around him at recess. "Mister Wellington boards in a room in our attic." He swore it was true. "We always have teachers staying at our house because we got extra room."

"What's it like?" Our eyes grew round as apples, all of us leaning in.

"He hardly says a word. My ma doesn't believe he talks all day long in the schoolhouse. He sits at our table for over an hour and none of us are allowed to leave until he's done."

"What's he doin' there so long?"

"Chewin'," Miles said. "Each mouthful, he chews one hundred times. Says it is good for digestion. He swallows so loud, the dog howls."

This set us all to giggling fits. We begged him for more. I never told those boys what I thought, or the stories I made up in my head about Mister Wellington. Only the girls heard them. They never made fun of me, and listened real close.

"Schoolmaster struts down the rows like a rooster, cockin' and crowin' with a puffed-up chest. A rooster that got old and too skinny, not worth cookin'," I told them.

"More! More!" they cheered.

"When he passes by the rows, everyone shivers like a bunch of hens waitin' for the axe to fall on their heads."

One girl laughed. "That's not funny! It's true."

We all snorted and sniggered until the bell rang. We had warmed ourselves by running, and laughed ourselves silly, but recess was over.

The only good part of that December was how many children stayed away from school. Outside, we were down to two boys and one girl. We heard Elmer had gone to Chatham with his family to look for jobs. Most other boys were off working with their fathers. I got the wall for the first time. My body hugged it tight. All day long, I clung to it, but not much heat came through now to melt the cold away.

Beulah was the only girl there. I wondered why she hadn't stayed home too. She needed coaxing to take the other side of the window though. It was her first chance at the wall and I told her she'd be safe.

"Nobody to stop you now," I said. "Best take it while you can."

She was younger than me, maybe seven, with dark scars down her left cheek. I didn't dare ask where they came from. I already knew. It came from slavery. She never said a word. Or ever laughed. Or wrote one letter. Only peeked through the window she was hiding behind with round eyes darting every way like she expected the Devil himself to show up.

Back home, there was a chicken that fell asleep on top a hay wagon and got knocked to the ground when it started up too fast. That chicken landed right on its head. Afterwards, it had to learn to eat and swallow all over again because it had forgotten how. It never laid eggs like the rest, just stayed by itself. That's what Beulah reminded me of.

I tried smiling at her some but she wouldn't smile back. So I took to whispering to her, explaining the letters *S, O, L* and *M*, the only ones I knew for sure. I just kept talking to her like we were having a conversation, though she never spoke back. Every single day afterwards, she kept near me, like my shadow.

So cold and damp, it seemed like fingers of ice prying beneath my clothes. We never saw a peek of sun for days and days. We all had tricks for dressing. Each piece of clothing I owned, from one holey sweater to a shirt, a woollen jacket, jeans, a scarf and a cap was piled on top of me. It was hard to run at recess in all those heavy clothes, but it gave comfort for an hour afterwards until the chills set in. But when that wind kicked up, blowing hard at our backs, we all shivered.

Inside, everyone took off their coats. Chairs began to empty there. Children got colds, fevers and whooping cough both inside and outside the classroom. Nobody came to fill the desks that had been empty when I began school. Betsy told me the truth, making me swear to tell no one. She said one of them belonged to her friend who moved away in September. The others never had students in them at all.

Whenever I looked inside the classroom, my eyes strayed to those empty seats, one of them right beside the wood stove. I wished I could sit there for one whole afternoon, peel off my coat and cap, lean back and sigh. But no one invited any of us in. So I pressed my body to the wall, refusing to look in.

This one day, I not only turned away but squeezed my ear flat to the wall too, drowning out the schoolmaster's voice. He was going on and on about multiplying numbers to make them bigger. I couldn't figure why anyone would bother to do such a thing. Soon I didn't hear a word he said. My eyes closed.

Pictures came. Heat. I remembered the Georgia heat. How I craved it now. Sunbright. I don't know if it was from dreaming or remembering, but I saw everything clear. *Grandpa whistled to me across the rows and rows of cotton. He knew when my fingers were scraped so raw, I wanted to cry and plop right down in the dirt. Couldn't do any such thing or it'd catch me a whipping. Again he whistled, cooling me from the bite of the cotton boll, just when my eyes felt like closing from the afternoon sun and my clothes were so soaked with sweat, they clung to me like second skin. Then his voice touched down like a breeze rustling the plants all around me in the middle of that nowhere field . . .*

When I opened my eyes, the schoolmaster's voice was still going on and on and the children were scratching away on their slates. Except for those outside. They saw it first. Beulah was hissing at me and pointing.

"Snow!" one boy whispered.

I'd been waiting and waiting for it. Any day now, the shopkeeper had said. Snow beat the air hard. Swirling left and right, up and down and sideways, it hit the air. Springing from nowhere, like a surprise. I pried myself away from the wall and walked out into the open air. I twirled in circles, dizzy. Leaned my head back, opened my mouth wide, and gulped down snow. Cool and fresh, it was the taste of Canada.

And then I cried. Tears stung my face, popping out quick as that snow. I was here in Canada. I was alive and safe. But I was not home. Grandpa couldn't see the first snow and laugh seeing me twirl in it. Nobody in the world cared what I did. Grandpa might never find us again. And I could not learn at all.

Beulah gave a warning hum and in the next second Mister Wellington had hold of my collar and set to thrashing my legs with his cane. Then he dragged me by the back of my jacket. When he was done, I was facing the corner inside the classroom.

I should have been embarrassed. But I was not. For I was

inside, right next to the wood stove. I unbuttoned my coat at last and sighed.

Of course Levi got to hear all about it because the schoolmaster marched me to the store right after school.

"Maybe if those children sat inside, right up front, they'd listen better to you, and not get sick from stayin' out in the cold," Levi said. "Any chance of that?"

Mister Wellington puckered his cheeks like he was going to spit. "You know the rules."

"We left such rules behind in Georgia," answered Levi. "That's why we risked our lives runnin' all the way here."

That evening, after dinner, news spread around the parlour about the Willis family over in Kent County, nearby.

"You heard about those two Willis children, a boy and his young sister, who left school because the other children picked on 'em?" one man asked.

"Nothin' new about that," another man said. "All kids do that."

"They were the only ones who weren't white like the teacher. But I hear it's worse, what happened next."

We all sat around the wood stove and heard how the schoolmaster expelled the two forever because they'd been away from school too many days. But the reason those children stayed away was because they were scared they'd get a beating from the white boys. Mr. Willis, the father, owned his own farm and paid taxes to send his children to school. So he marched his children back to school. Schoolmaster refused to let them in. And nobody in town did anything at all about it.

"That man Willis is sellin' his farm and movin' on."

"Can't blame him," sighed Levi. "Where are we gonna find a place that will welcome us? And let us have our own lives too."

"Maybe we got to stick with our own kind. Like those settlements I hear about where coloured folk own land: Dawn, Buxton, Wilberforce. All are nearby. I hear they are fine spots if you are willin' to work hard. And have some start-up money."

It got late. Levi sent me to our room to memorize the multiplication tables for homework. I wanted to hear the men tell about the settlements. Bet they were like Little Africa, where we would be safe and there'd be real families there. So I lingered where they could not see me on the top of the stairwell and listened as Levi went on and on. A long time later, as my eyes drooped, I sat up straight and listened to him.

"Even in Canada, I'm still runnin'. Afraid to let Jacob down, I suppose. He was one of the elders. Everyone looked up to him. He put me in charge of Sol. Then he had to stay behind. Ever since, I bury myself in work. That way I don't think too hard."

"About what?"

"Hidin' and scoutin' – that's easy to do. But what do I know about raisin' a boy? I don't know how to tell him — " Levi paused. I flattened to the floor and held my breath. " — what to tell him about his grandpa. I'll have to tell him someday. Sol will hate me for it. So I don't say much to him at all. And he's so quiet sometimes."

"What you got to say about his grandpa? Is he all right?"

"Most likely, Sol won't be seeing his grandpa. Ever. Besides a busted ankle, he may have broken a hip. Old slaves don't mend well. They break down, like my pa Enos."

My body went still like a deep well. Levi's words echoed down inside me. Now I knew what kept Levi running, even here in this new land. Now I knew what he knew — Grandpa might never come over to this side of the river.

I could barely breathe. It felt like I'd been kicked in the stomach. So I kicked back. One hard boot to the wall before running to our room.

Tossing and turning, l fumed like a wood stove burning wet wood. It wasn't true. Grandpa *was* coming back. Didn't I hear his voice tell me so? But I'd heard it only twice since we separated. *Wait on me, Solomon*, was what I heard last. Not another word after that.

It was pitch dark when Levi plopped onto his cot, hands behind his head, looking up at the ceiling. He caught me watching him. My homework was not done. And my jaw was set about not doing it too. I would never forgive him for what he said about Grandpa.

But Levi surprised me. He got to talking. "All our lives as slaves, we have been on the outside just like that Willis family. In Bloomfield School, you are still on the outside," he said. "Only difference is that now you are allowed to look in. That's not good enough for your grandpa. Or me."

It was the first time Levi spoke to me like this, truth-telling, as if I were a man and not some boy. It was then I suddenly remembered I must have turned twelve some time over the summer. So I dared speak up and tell what I thought. "The Willis school sounds worse than mine. Maybe everywhere is like this. Besides, I'm not learnin'. None of us children like the schoolmaster, no matter what colour we are."

Levi frowned. "That school is no good. And I earn less than I did in Little Africa. No better job around this town. This is not the place to settle down in, like I'd hoped. Where do we go from here though? I don't know. But we got to go."

In the dark, a smile lit my face for the first time since we stopped in Raleigh Township. We're moving on again because

Levi said so. I was glad through and through this time. There was nothing I was leaving behind. I'd miss some girls is all. Betsy's smile and how she twirled like an angel in that dress. Maybe Beulah would have told me her story if I'd stayed on longer. Something had stilled her, same as me. Now I would miss the chance of ever hearing her speak.

But if I never went to school again, it'd be too soon for me. At least Levi could swear to Grandpa how I tried to learn in two different schools. Wasn't that near enough the truth?

Chapter 20
BY THE THAMES

Late December 1857

BEST THING ABOUT LEVI IS, once he says he's going, his feet start walking. Not like some who sit around all day talking. Lucky for me, he was starting to think my way.

"The job comes first. We need money to buy a farm," he decided. "Then we can think about sendin' you to school."

Levi had a plan. He'd spoken to Elmer's family before they left. So, like them, he planned to head into Chatham, some four miles away. He just kept moving on and never talked about looking for Grandpa anymore. If Levi had said one word about him, I would have started begging to go back to Bertie Hall. But still, I had to be thankful. Bloomfield was at our backs. I'd never have to see that schoolhouse again. I didn't mind where Levi went this time. We were like Canada's winter wind, blowing everywhere.

Stories had spread about Chatham. How coloured folk had banded together there to save a young boy from being snapped up by slavecatchers. They told how a woman named Shadd, who'd been born free, snatched the boy from their hands and ran all the way to the courthouse with him to ring the bells. The whole town — not just the whites, but everybody — came running and chased the slavecatchers right out of town.

Chatham was a proper town. It was busy with more folks than I'd ever seen, and lots of them were our kind, but rich. Some even wore Sunday clothes in the middle of the week. Tall brick buildings lined the main street, with wooden walkways out front, to keep your feet out of the mud (and worse things, after the horses had been by). Carriages rolled down streets. The Thames River ran behind town. We headed right to it. Our bellies were growling by then. We'd eaten only cornbread that morning and now was our chance to fish.

But the river was frozen. Levi grabbed boulders and flung them down in one spot. I leaned over and stuck a branch in the hole he was making to clean out more ice. The ice wasn't that thick after all. Deep down, there was grey water.

Levi and I pulled out the string and hooks we still had from living by the lake. Lucky we had stale cornbread for bait. Plunked it down through the ice and squatted. Here and there along the riverbank, as dusk came on, other folks plopped down to fish.

I shouted out to Levi when I saw someone yank up a fish opposite us. "Perch!"

"Sssh! Got to be quiet to catch 'em," Levi reminded me. "Fishin' and thinkin' go together. Been a long while since I did either one."

In the stillness, as it grew darker, we sat and watched. Levi seemed far away, staring down into the river. We had to catch fish or there'd be no dinner. So I didn't dare say a word. Just rocked back and forth, trying to keep warm. But what I heard next made me hold my breath.

The call of the whippoorwill drifted by.

Faint and mournful. Four beats: whip-po-or-will! Out of season. Death song.

I looked along the riverbank where other families fished. There were white folks too, with their poles sunk in the river. Nearby was a bridge, but no sign of the night bird. Mist rose like a cloud from one spot, near a pile of stones. Vapour twirled and swirled into a shape almost like a person. Again, the bird sang: whip-po-or-will!

I've been brushed by death just now, I thought. *Another ghost has appeared.* I shivered as the icy coldness of the ground shot right through me. Suddenly Levi yanked up a fish, breaking the spell I was in.

"Fine catch!" a man said, sitting down to join us. "Name is Will."

By full dark, between the three of us, we had a pile of perch and bass. I didn't even joke about it being Levi's first catch. My mouth wouldn't work at all. We were all shivering by then and there was no shelter anywhere. The three of us had no home to go to, so we built a fire and roasted our fish right there. I sat right up close and let the flames nearly touch me. What I had just seen by the river, I kept quiet about.

"I'm on my way to Bloomfield," Will told us. "Christmas is soon. Left my daughter with a family there who promised she'd get her schoolin'."

"Solomon will know her then," said Levi. "We just come from Bloomfield."

"Beulah's her name."

At that name, I smiled right away.

Will immediately asked me, "How is my girl doin'?"

I thought of Beulah hugging the wall, loving shadows. "Oh, she listens close to the schoolmaster."

"Is she talkin'?"

I shook my head. Beulah had been like me after all, without family, on her own.

"Poor child. I should never have left her so long," Will said. "A year has passed. Took me time to earn some money and come back for her. Maybe I needed time to forget, too, so I could begin over."

"Why don't the girl talk?" Levi asked.

That question hung in the air like a buzzing mosquito.

"Whip caught her young — at six — when they pushed her to the fields. She didn't move fast enough. Got lashes on her face and up and down her back too. That's what made me decide we should run. That would have been enough to quiet any young girl, but what happened next was worse."

Those long, dark scars across her whole cheek I saw when I first met Beulah. The whip must have lashed out hard to cut her so deep.

Will looked down at his shoes. "Beulah's ma and our new baby boy got sick with fever in the woods. I lit out for a doctor. Gone overnight. By the time I got back, they both passed away. Beulah saw it all. The two of us kept runnin' after that. Beulah cried for months. When she was done cryin', she was done talkin' too."

Such a silence came over us, like a dark cloud passing by, making me shiver.

"I got to be with Beulah now. We'll settle in Bloomfield for a while."

Levi looked at me. It was like the two of us were talking with just our eyes. Bloomfield School was no place for Beulah.

Other fishermen joined us around our fire by then. Some had landed at Long Point or Port Burwell, off big ships from Ohio. One man said he swam across the Detroit River with his belongings on his back. Most of them had been living in Chatham for some time. A few had families and houses of their own in the east end of town. Some had jobs blacksmithing, bricklaying or doing carpentry for the ships. One, Isaac, was a butcher who owned his own store. Levi whistled when he heard how the men's trades back home had brought them good jobs here.

"We all got our start here," Isaac said. "Must be a thousand of us in Chatham now. We stick together. Just last August, two fancy slavecatchers arrived at the Royal Exchange Hotel in town to bring a new arrival, Alexander, back into slavery."

"Did they take him away?" Will asked.

Isaac shook his head. "A crowd of us gathered round to hear the story. Alexander called those men liars and murderers. Said he was free and had done no wrong. That was enough for us. We escorted those white men to the train. Never saw them again."

I saw how Levi sighed at the end of that story.

Then suddenly one of the fishermen asked, "You're not afraid to be out at night near Water Street?"

Isaac poked him. "Watch what you say. There's a young boy here."

"This boy?" joked Will. "He's been through slavery. What can be worse than that? You gonna tell us what happened close by?"

"Those who ran north first came here around 1815," said the man. "Folks in Chatham never saw so many people from the South before, all homeless, livin' by the river. More runaways joined them each month. They'd seen slaves trailin' owners, but never so many free and livin' in their town. Then one night a young boy, about fifteen, disappeared."

"Murdered!" said another.

Will, Levi and I gasped.

"Here, at the end of Water Street, right by that root cellar over there, some say they catch sight of him. Say his body is buried there. Nobody found him and no one was charged with the crime, though they suspected a white man killed him. That boy haunts this river for dyin' like he did."

We all looked to where the man pointed. Shivers rolled through me before I even turned my gaze. It was exactly where I'd seen that vapour. Never guessed it was a boy. Good thing I never saw his face clear. Good thing he was on the far riverbank.

Two boys, both ghosts, had appeared to me near water — Rodney, drowned, and now this other boy, likely killed by a white man. Nobody else saw them but me. I sure didn't want to see such things. Or the blood that kept dripping in my nightmares. Even the ghosts of Beulah's mother and brother lingered in the air like the whippoorwill's cry. I remembered Grannie saying hauntings happen near a place when death comes too quick and too soon.

Everyone was silent for a long while, thinking about that mournful story.

"Some folks didn't want us around here back then," said the man who told us the story. "Some still don't. Yet we keep comin' anyway. Sure is a whole lot better than livin' in the South."

"Abolitionists welcome us here and buy from my shop," Isaac said. "There's also the church in town that helps newcomers get settled. You three been there yet?"

"Where's it at?" Levi asked.

It was getting late by then. The moon had been up for hours. Most of the other fishermen were long gone home. The men rose to stretch and yawn, flinging their catch over their shoulders. Tomorrow, Levi decided, we'd go to the church with Will. But we had nowhere to go now.

I was afraid we'd spend the night sleeping by the riverbank. I wouldn't get a wink of sleep. We'd be facing the reminder of death across the way.

Isaac invited the three of us to stay the night in his house a short walk away on King Street East.

"Got a pretty flower garden out front come spring. My wife's doin'," he said. "Out back, there's two young apple trees and a garden of vegetables each summer. For now, we can give you a warm fire for the night."

Levi and Will agreed right away. "Wouldn't miss the chance to stay inside a house *owned* by a man who was once a slave. It'll be our first time."

He had given the best answer. It was getting to be that Levi and I were of the same mind.

Chapter 21
CROSSING BACK

Late December 1857

NEXT MORNING, WE HEADED to the BME Church, where some women invited us to sit down. They served us hot buckwheat porridge, bacon and apples, just because we were newcomers in Chatham. Welcome breakfast, they called it. It heated me through and through. I could barely speak after sensing that ghost by the river last night, but Levi was grinning like he had found gold.

Everyone who came in was raggedy like us, in need of a scrubbing, a shave, a haircut and new clothes. The two children there were thin as kindling sticks. They had been on the road for four months, their pa said, and just arrived in Canada. One old man fell asleep waiting. But what was most surprising was how one man in a clean shirt and pants and some women in good dresses appeared to call each family over, one by one. Not only that, but they could read and write, for they wrote the people's names down on paper. At last it was our turn to be seen.

"We were once runaways too," the man in the clean shirt said as he shook our hands. "I've been here seven years. That's my wife over there. We're members of The True Band, an organization across Canada that helps those comin' into this country get settled. You heard of us?"

Levi and Will both shook their heads.

"You want work?" he asked. "You could go to the mills where they take all these trees the men are clearin'. Fifteen years ago, they say this place was wilderness. Now it's all changin'. Come spring, when the river melts, there's work unloadin' boats."

Will and Levi looked at one another.

"Can you tell us about a good place to settle with children?" asked Levi. "Got to have a good school and a place to farm both."

"Chatham has some schools for our people only. Princess Street School is nearby. Not sure if the children learn there. So overcrowded. Only a few go on to high school. But farmland around here is costly. Why don't you go up to the settlements?"

Levi spoke up. "We met some folks who were just steppin' off a boat into Canada. They were headed straight to Dawn."

"Why don't you head to Buxton? I have relatives there and they are pleased," answered the man. "Run by a white man, a reverend, but people who go there from the South own their own land. Otherwise, they can't stay on. And you don't need much money."

I thought about how those folks we met went up to Dawn. They walked with shiny faces and quick feet to get there. I had wanted to join them. What happened to them, we would never know.

Will leaned in. "How much do we need for buyin' land in Buxton?"

"Two and a half dollars an acre. It's fertile land with plenty of timber. You pay a small yearly fee for ten years and a down payment. Then you own it clear. The land was bought by abolitionists to help folks get settled. Won't find cheaper or better land anywhere."

Levi blinked. He had nearly fifty dollars saved in his pocket.

"And the schools?" Levi asked. "Bet they didn't think of that."

The man smiled. "Indeed, they did think of that. Plenty. Folks say it has the best schools around. Its graduates have gone on to Toronto to become teachers and doctors."

"You seen it over in those settlements?" Levi turned to Will.

"Passed through Buxton last year. I'd say it was prosperin'. Everyone's workin'. Plenty of houses. About eight hundred people live around there. Hay already cut in June."

Levi's eyes widened. He stood straight up. All eyes landed on him. It was one of those moments when everything seemed to slow down to a stop.

Let's go there, my heart pumped. *Let's go up to Buxton.*

Levi's chest widened with air like he was full to the brim. "Sol and I are goin' to Buxton!" he announced. "What about you, Will?"

Will smiled. "Figure the best I can do is take Beulah up to Buxton with you. There's a family feelin' there, I bet. Maybe other young girls like her. The money I saved clearin' land will buy us our own plot. We'll settle down to a farm too."

The air busted out of me. Suddenly I began to laugh and jump all around that church. I even whooped up some. Nobody seemed to mind. Least of all Levi and Will, who were busy marking *X*s for their signatures on papers, signing up for Buxton and hearing directions about how to get there. The man said they'd send word ahead to the settlement to expect us. Maybe there'd even be berry pie waiting for us, I imagined.

"Our luck has got to change in Buxton," said Levi. "Maybe if we set our feet down in one place, we'll grow roots."

That's what I'd been trying to tell Levi for the longest time. But even if I had tugged hard on his sleeve day and night, he'd never have listened to me. Back in Little Africa, some days

128

there'd be a feeling of belonging to Canada as I ran over its ground, so flat and free. Underneath my feet, the country felt alive. And so did I, for the very first time. Strong enough and wild enough to race the trains. Was that feeling true? Maybe in Buxton it'd happen again.

But first we had to cross back to Bloomfield to get Beulah. We fished some more that day, cooked it up and stayed on with Isaac. Two days later, with supplies we got in town from The True Band, we headed off. In my backpack was a used pair of pants with no holes, and extra shoelaces for Grandpa and me. Will owned a horse and wagon and we piled on board for the trip. We arrived at Bloomfield in the dark. I held still in the back of the wagon while Will went inside the house where Beulah had been living. Not long afterwards, Beulah walked out with a sack of clothes in one hand, the other hand in her pa's. She was crying. Even her tears were silent and slow. As she passed by the back of the wagon, her eyes lit on me and grew wide in wonderment.

"Solomon!"

That word rang in the air, my own name on her lips. Everyone stared. Beulah's pa gasped. I laughed out loud, thinking how my own name once brought me into a heap of trouble at the schoolhouse, and now it brought Beulah to speak.

I reached out my hand to pull her inside and began talking words at her in a rush, telling her how we were all going up to Buxton together. By the time Beulah was stuffing roasted perch in her mouth, we had passed the schoolhouse by. I chanted "Good riddance!" to it in my best shouting voice. We even stuck our tongues out at it. Us two were rolling in the back of the wagon while the men sat up front, like one big family.

Levi started singing a song and we all joined in to call and clap and beat our feet hard on the floorboards, crossing the back roads of Raleigh Township.

I can't stay behind, my Lord,
I can't stay behind!
There's room enough, room enough,
room enough in heaven, my Lord;
Room enough, room enough,
I can't stay behind.

The fishermen said we'd get to Buxton faster if we took Duck Pond Road. It would keep us out of the creeks and rivers that trickled everywhere; it'd be the shortest way. So we took that road through the dark night, not seeing much. Beulah and I kept rolling all over inside the wagon.

In the middle of that night, Will yelled to his horse, awakening us. We ground to a stop and pitched to one side. The wagon fell on its side, wheels spinning in air.

"You all right in there?" Levi called. "We're stuck. This spell of warm weather made the ice melt. Below us is all mud and rotting trees. We're in some kind of swamp."

It took some heaving to get the wagon back up and coax the horse to keep walking. It slipped and slid over the half-frozen earth. Up and down, that poor horse sunk into holes and then struggled to rise up again. Will lifted Beulah up onto his shoulders while Levi and I walked behind, steering the wagon straight and even pushing it at times. Beulah's dark eyes bulged out of her thin, scarred face. Her head was turning in all directions. She'd been through swamps on the underground before. Bet she was checking for snakes.

Then I remembered the swamp in Georgia. We had wandered into it weeks after we took the underground road.

Seemed like a dream to me now. I could see Levi lifting me high up on his shoulders to keep me dry. I seemed like a young boy back then, though it was only nine months ago. When new troubles appeared on the underground, they got piled on top old troubles and stacked up so high, it seemed there'd be no end to trouble.

Back in that Georgia swamp, Grandpa had insisted, "Nobody's ever gonna follow us through this swamp. They'll lose our trail. We'll get through fine."

I remembered how Grandpa Jacob's voice lit the gloom as we sunk in that mud. His voice matched the rest of him — steady. All my growing up years, I wished to be like him. And we did get through, just like he said, stepping onto higher ground next day.

There was no sign of snakes in this swamp. It was winter and most likely such creatures would be sleeping. Or hiding with all the racket we were making.

"We'll get through fine," I yelled to Beulah. "Can't be any worse than sittin' still and copyin' out *The Canada Spelling Book* under Mister Wellington's nose."

She looked down at me with her lips set in a pout and studied my smile starting up. Hours later, I heard her call. "Look! We're out of the mud. Sol was right."

That's how I knew I had a piece of Grandpa in me. He always saw far ahead, past all our troubles, where I could never see until that very moment. "After so much darkness," he always said, "got to be sun-up somewhere."

Beulah and I climbed into the back of the wagon at last and lay down. Our eyes shut. It was already daybreak. Soon we'd be in Buxton. Soon . . .

If only Grandpa would come find me there, I thought. That's all I wanted since I crossed over.

Chapter 22
COMING INTO THE NEW WORLD

Buxton, January 1858

THE AFTERNOON WE RODE INTO BUXTON, we knew we had come into a new world, a place we could never have imagined. It was a busy town in the middle of the woods. At a crossroads in the centre of town where we stopped for directions, a couple named the buildings for us: hotel, post office, school, church, blacksmith shop, shoe shop and general store. Everywhere, people were walking, driving wagons and riding horses. Some dressed in fine clothes. Everyone going someplace. Seemed to be hundreds of people around.

We stopped at St. Andrew's Presbyterian Church where we told a man our story of coming into Canada.

"Welcome!" He was beaming at us. "Always room here for more. You come to the right place with these young ones. Though Buxton's school is overflowin', they'll welcome you. I'll send word to expect two new students first thing in the mornin'."

Levi said, "Sir, we have come to buy land and farm it. When can we start?"

"Reverend King is the one to ask; he makes the rules here and sells land. Meanwhile, you can all get settled, a few miles north up this road. That's where we're sendin' newcomers now. The girl and her pa can stay with a widow there and help her out; you and your boy will sleep at a cabin just built."

"How long can we stay in these homes?" asked Will.

"'Til spring. By then, you will have a dwellin' of your own.

We'll make sure of that. We all pitch in here. Folks in your neighbourhood will invite you to dinner tonight. But first I must tell everyone you have arrived."

"Well, I hear there's plenty of people around here," said Will. "How are you gonna tell 'em all?"

"Wait a few minutes while I go into the church. Give a listen for four signals. One hundred and eighty families live here and they'll all want to rejoice with you."

We stood on the path while the man disappeared inside.

Will laughed and pointed to the very top of the church. "Is he gonna climb to the top of that steeple to wave a handkerchief and shout to the whole town?"

In the next minute came our answer. One gong of a bell so loud Beulah and I flew to the road and covered our ears. It pulsed out of the church from way up high.

Will announced, "That bell's callin' my name!"

Folk passing by looked over at us and waved.

"Welcome to Buxton!" one called out.

Another yelled, "How does it feel to be free?"

Shouts and laughter surrounded us. Then another bell sounded.

Levi got caught up in the excitement. "I am free!" he screamed to all the people around.

Beulah and I doubled back to the church. It was still shaking with the toll of the last bell. It would be our turn next. So I leaned against the church and Beulah squeezed right beside me. The hard church wall was flat against my back when the next bell sounded. *Rinnnnng!*

"This bell is sayin' *Sol-o-mon!*" I called out.

The wall was a like a living heartbeat. Seemed it could bust the whole church apart with its joyful racket. When the last bell gonged, with it came Beulah's scream of "Me-e-e-e! Beu-lah!"

My ears were popping and the bones in my body were all shaking by then. Will and Levi twirled around in circles in the middle of the street.

"It's a new day!" yelled Will. "Though I have lived in Canada some time, it's not until this moment that I feel free."

"Since we crossed over, we been runnin' like rabbits," Levi gasped. "But here we are surrounded by people who used to be slaves like us, and they're all comin' out to welcome us!"

A tall white man walked over, dressed all in black except for a white shirt that shone so bright it hurt my eyes to look at it. "We do notice you and rejoice with you, son. Every time a newcomer enters Buxton, we celebrate by ringing the church bells. They say folks can hear the Liberty Bell over in Chatham. You are the reason we built this community — to help you find a home. "

We all stopped to stare at this man.

A passerby called out to him, "Reverend King, we soon will have all the slaves of the South livin' in freedom in Canada!"

Levi and Will took off their caps and immediately bowed. They introduced themselves and spoke about hoping to buy land. The Reverend nodded his grey head and promised to meet with them tomorrow. Then he called Beulah and me to come close.

He was tall as an August beanpole and pink-skinned. I had to gaze way up in the sky to see him. He looked through me and seemed to know all there was to know. Once a slave boy. Abandoned by all — mother, father, grandfather. Without any learning. And no heart to learn. In an instant he knew it all, even what I kept from everyone — how I wanted to bolt many times on our journey and run back to the place we crossed over, just to see if Grandpa was coming. Just to find the lost part of me I left over there with him. But Reverend King's eyes kept searching deeper, as if he thought he'd find more to me.

"You will do well here, son," he said. "Your mind needs to grow to keep up with your body. In all ways, you will find nourishment here. Keep a watch on this little girl too. She needs a friend such as you."

Something was running out of me like a river. Though I stood at attention and listened, it felt right calm to be looking at this Reverend. It was like he knew some secret that I did not know. I hoped Buxton would be a home and that Levi wouldn't get itchy feet to roam again. Maybe, if we stayed in one spot, Grandpa would find us. There'd be no ghosts here, either. It was all too new.

Along the main road, called Centre Road, we passed more big buildings. A sawmill and brickyard, we were told by the man who rode with us to show us around. On each side of the road sat the settlers' sawn-log cabins, and a few frame houses washed white and gleaming like the snow piled up high everywhere, all set back from the road, in line with one another. The main road was rough and bumpy, full of gnarled tree roots that our horse kept tripping over.

It was dark by the time the man left us at our new neighbours' cabin. Inside was warm and it glowed from lamplight. A table was set with real plates and around it sat a big family with young ones and an elder. A woman named Jenny invited us to sit while she set out two more plates and carried in trays of steaming hot food. I admit I remember nothing much of what was said. What I recall most was the venison meat in a heap on my plate and its sweet smokiness. And the men's laughter as they watched it disappear in my mouth in one minute. And someone saying, "You are most welcome in Buxton. Anythin' you need to start up here, you just ask us."

Afterwards, we settled in our own cabin. It smelled of new pine wood inside, freshly sawed. Empty with no shutters on the windows. A wash basin on a stand with a water pitcher in the first room. Fireplace with a low fire burning. No furniture except for two beds in separate rooms, one of which was all mine.

No sooner had we looked around when Levi and I heard a low hum of voices. Outside, pine torches were held high and wavered in a long line. For a moment I thought we were back on the plantation. It made my heart stand still. Dozens of folks were travelling along the path. We stood and watched by the window. No one stopped. One by one, more torches passed by and disappeared. Back home, there'd been camp meetings too. In winter, when dark comes early, slaves would sneak off to the woods to pray or dance. There'd been secret meetings too about running on the underground. I never went off to one, but I sure heard folks singing about it in the fields, telling one another about the meeting that night. Lines began to sing in my head, words I'd heard since I was a child.

There's a fire in the east. There's a fire in the west.
There's a meetin' here tonight.
Camp meetin' down in the wilderness.

"Where are they goin'?" I whispered to Levi as the last torch flickered.

He shrugged. "Only one way to find out. Follow 'em. See you in the mornin', Sol. Go to sleep now if you plan on gettin' to that school early."

136

With that, Levi went out the door, leaving me behind. Was it safe to be all alone when everyone else went off somewhere? I peered outside again. Jenny's cabin was already dark. Here and there in the distance, candles shone in some windows.

But then the memories creeped inside like a stranger into an empty house and found me all alone. I never invited them in. But they came anyway. I remembered hearing from Grandpa about my own pa going to such meetings in the woods. Secret meetings held late at night. They were the reason Pa never came back. And never said goodbye either. How many nights I'd lie awake, hoping to hear word of him, I wouldn't tell.

I climbed into my very own bed then and piled a pillow on top my head, but all that silence hummed around me. The room seemed so high, with empty spaces everywhere and nothing to fill it. In the morning I'd be sent to school, forever this time. Levi had forgotten all about finding Grandpa.

In the new quiet, I remembered the night we left him. Him saying he didn't know how long it was going to take. The sharp look in Levi's eyes, and Grandpa looking away from me. After that, Levi and I scattered like fallen leaves across Canada. Nobody kept track of where we were. How exactly were we going to meet up here? An old man like Grandpa could never follow us so far. Besides, Levi said he wouldn't be coming back. Ever. Such a thing I never wanted to think of, so I pushed it into the far back of my mind.

A shiver shot right through me like a knife.

That last night I saw him, Grandpa promised he'd meet me on the other side. Then he waved his arm high and never looked back. But . . . he didn't mean the other side of the Niagara River at all. Or Canada. He was speaking of *heaven*, when surely we'd see everybody again. And then I feared the truth: Grandpa wasn't coming back to me anymore. Not in this life.

One by one, I lost them all. Ma. Pa. Grandpa Jacob.

Why couldn't I hold onto you, Grandpa?

The two of us ran to be free, to find someplace safe. I finally got to Buxton and he didn't. He'd never see me grow now, or learn my letters. He was gone for good.

Grandpa! Why did you leave me?

I slipped beneath the wooden bed, my back to the floor, and yanked tight on the slats above my head. My feet started kicking the bed and the floor and that set my arms to yanking and my voice let loose wailing. You could probably hear it clear across Canada, but I didn't care.

Chapter 23
BUXTON MISSION SCHOOL

THE BELLS RANG OVER AND OVER in the still dark January morning. I sat up in bed and felt them pulse through my whole body, waking me up from head to toe. Can a newly freed slave have come into Buxton so early?

Then I remembered. Around the dinner table last night, Jenny's family had told us to listen for the bells twice a day, marking our early rising and dinnertime. They had told us the reason for their tolling then, but I guess I forgot.

I stood up and wiggled into my old clothes. Some new clothes by the bedside looked like Sunday clothes, so smooth and clean. I wondered whose they were and whose cabin this was. The owners were nowhere around. Levi ordered me to wash my face. He frowned at my boots with their bottoms flapping open and swore to fix them that night.

"Wasn't that something to eat venison last night?" he asked as we chewed on Jenny's leftover corn pones. "Never expected to be tastin' Buxton potatoes either. Dee-lish-ee-us! I can't wait to get started farmin' my own land. Raise some chickens too."

The two of us walked along a path to Centre Road, then the two miles back to the schoolhouse. The closer we got, the slower my feet moved. Levi was going on and on about his meeting that day with Reverend King. Then I suddenly remembered the torches and him going out in the dark.

"What happened last night at that meetin'?" I asked.

139

"You wouldn't believe it. That Reverend teaches school at night to folks busy workin' all day. They seemed to read some. And do sums too."

I gasped. "Grown men and women goin' to school?"

"Now I know why you didn't like Bloomfield School. Sounded like they were speakin' in strange tongues. But everythin' is different here, Solomon. Maybe school will be too. Something brand new about this place. I feel our luck changin'."

With that he left me at the Mission School, right between the church and the cemetery. Behind it was Mr. King's big log house with many trees in front. That's where Levi headed. We had walked through the dark to get there early, and when the sun broke through, the schoolhouse shone white as a cloud. Straight as the Presbyterian Church. Boys and girls, of all colours, came from the woods and roads, skipping and chattering. We gathered on the road until the bells called. All the children stopped playing then, ran over to the schoolhouse where a man stood ringing a bell, and lined up in front of him.

From out of nowhere, a hand slipped into mine. Beulah fixed her dark eyes on mine and I squeezed her hand tight. I'd have to be on the lookout for her, Reverend King had told me. But I was the one right glad to have someone I knew beside me among all those strangers.

We rushed to the line. I craned my neck all around to look for another building or lean-to. But the only one close by was the outhouse out back. Surely they didn't mean to put us in there. There was no separate line for us and whites either. Just one for boys and one for girls. Then I looked at the schoolmaster standing at the top of the steps. He was dressed in a fine grey suit, not too tall or too short. He filled out his suit with a full chest. He stared down at all of us and waited until everyone got still. And I stared back with an open mouth. For the schoolmaster was brown as me.

"Good morning, children!" he called out. "Are you ready for school today?"

"Good mornin', Mister Dillon! Indeed, we are," they answered him.

The students walked inside silently, with Beulah and me at the rear. Everyone settled in their places. The teacher gave us a seat and desk in the middle of the crowded classroom. Children of all ages were in that room. Side by side, we sat down with over a hundred children, some who looked as young as five while others were my age or older.

First, morning hymns and some Scripture reading by one of the oldest students. This set me wondering. Was he from the South like me and how had he learned so quick in this school-house? Then the schoolmaster began to read from the Bible. He told a story of how one sheep got lost and the shepherd left his whole flock and went in search of that one stray sheep. I thought it wrong to leave the sheep unguarded until I heard how the man finally found the lost sheep and carried him back while the rest of the sheep waited safely. I breathed a sigh of relief along with Beulah.

"You, class, were lost sheep," the schoolmaster told us. "Some of you wandered here from a thousand miles off. Some of your parents carried you or birthed you here. You all rose up from slavery to freedom. You have been lost, ignored, mistreat-ed. But you have crossed over. The education in this class and teachings in the church will return you to the flock." He walked up and down the rows with a picture of Jesus, the shepherd, holding the one lost sheep in his arms as he joined the herd.

The schoolmaster stopped at my desk. "Here in Buxton, you all know that we ring the Liberty Bell whenever a freedom seeker crosses over. We all heard the four bells yesterday afternoon. Indeed, two newly free ones are sitting amongst us."

One of the boys near me had told me as soon as I sat down that morning to write my name on my slate if I knew how. I wanted to roll my eyes at him. That lesson I had surely learned the hard way.

"Solomon!" Mister Dillon looked down at my slate. "A boy who recently crossed over and already he writes his own name."

Just yesterday Levi was so amazed at the welcoming we got by the church. Even Reverend King said how everyone here in Buxton rejoiced with us. Now it felt like bells were ringing inside me, calling my name out, all those long letters, a name I was no longer embarrassed by, "Sol-o-mon!" I heard my own name ring like the Liberty Bell.

I sat straight up. I had planned on being invisible like back in Bloomfield School. Instead, my name was sounding around the room and it made me look straight at the schoolmaster and follow him with both my eyes and heart.

Then he continued. "And this is the newly arrived girl. What is your name, child?"

The silence was so stifling that I had to loosen my collar. My heart began to bang in my chest for fear of what would happen next. If Beulah didn't speak now, she might never speak to the schoolmaster. Didn't I know the pain of never speaking up for myself? I dared turn my head to stare at her.

Remember, I wanted to say out loud. *Remember how you spoke to me just yesterday.*

Her eyes shifted my way. She swallowed loudly.

"I am . . . Beulah, sir."

"Welcome to you, Beulah, and your friend Solomon, too."

Beulah sat bolt upright and kept her eyes upon the schoolmaster just as I did.

Afterwards, while the students copied a passage from the Bible onto their slate, Mister Dillon walked down the rows for inspection. If he came by your desk, you immediately stood and held out your hands and sleeves for him to inspect, then turned your head to show your neck and collar. As he walked closer and closer to me, my breath pulled shorter and shorter. Beulah leaned far back in her chair like a mouse watching a cat.

His shoes stopped right at my desk. Up I stood straight as I could and held out my hands. Mister Dillon pondered me. He looked long at me, as if viewing me from a distance, then his eyes fixed in close on the speck that was me. Or rather the specks of dirt that were all over me. I followed his eyes and saw in dread my ragged fingernails, dirt-filled and long, and my cuffs blackened with months of wearing. Who knows what he saw on my neck or collar, for he stared there a while. When I turned to face him, I saw his shiny wavy hair combed down flat and neat.

"Welcome to Buxton Mission School, Solomon. Tell us where you came from."

"Georgia, Mister Dillon."

"Solomon, at this school students must all look gleaming. Polished like the best silver. Tomorrow you know how you must come to school. Fingernails trimmed and hands scrubbed. Hair combed. A clean shirt. Your boots fixed."

I looked right into his wide eyes beneath their long eyebrows. He had seen everything. Even the loose flapping of my soles.

"Yes, sir," I promised. And though he moved on, his presence lingered all around me like some flower's scent. I saw myself in clean clothes and polished hands tomorrow, looking like the schoolmaster himself.

To Beulah I heard him say, "Welcome! Such an alert girl. I know you will return tomorrow freshly scrubbed. Do you have someone at home to help you?"

Beulah nodded.

"Who do you live with?" he asked her.

A long pause. "My . . . I live with my pa, sir."

That made all the air leave my lungs and fill them up again.

"Good. Then you must tell him we expect cleanliness."

Soon after that, he switched Beulah's seat and mine to way up front. Emanuel, the boy who had read that morning, sat between us. He'd be our monitor; he'd help us with our lessons. Better than that was what sat by my right elbow: the wood stove. I had dared take my coat off and hang it in the cloakroom with all the rest that morning. Good thing I did, for now I felt like toast warming on an oven.

After studying how big the world was and how full of great lakes Canada was, Mister Dillon showing us maps and pictures so blue with water, we drew our own map of this free country. The long narrow stretch of sandy shore we'd walked to get here, laying on top of Lake Erie. Below it was the country we fled from. All that lake water, deep and wide, lapping between the free and those still in slavery. We were far away from danger. How easy it was to draw the land so solid and covered in snow and colour the water a deep blue. As I looked around the classroom, I admired how my drawing was just as good as those of the other students who sat around me.

Maybe I could read someday too. Maybe the words could

run past my eyes like water flowing downhill, quick as a water-fall, the way Emanuel read that morning. He never paused or stumbled like most students in Bloomfield School. Never needed correction. Just rolled those words on his tongue as if they tasted as delicious as Buxton's potatoes. And Mister Dillon saying "Mmm" and nodding his head while he listened to Emanuel's words. Just like he did to the sound of my very own name.

Chapter 24
BETWEEN THE TOMBSTONES

February 1858

WHEN WE GOT BACK TO OUR CABIN late one afternoon, a mahogany-skinned woman was waiting for us, carrying a basket in her arms. She handed it to Levi.

"I'm Isabella, one of your neighbours," she told us. "I left you clothes and clean sheets. I can do your washin' come Saturdays, and cookin' too. No time for you to do such things when you're workin' all day. Let me do it. Most folks pay what they can."

She was plump and tall with checkered skirts that swished, and a way of smiling that spread over her whole face. Seemed quick to laugh. Not like us. She smelled of soap and fresh air, just like the clothes left in my room.

"We've been livin' in the woods too long," Levi told her. "So you got to excuse our manners. We sure appreciated the welcome you left." He took a big whiff of the basket. "Mmm! Do I smell roasted chicken? If this is how you cook, then we sure want you to work for us."

Isabella smiled, and nodded her head. "Dumplings. And cornbread too. I can bring you such food each evenin'."

I was hungry as a cottonmouth slithering out on the first spring day. I thought I was doomed forever to Levi's crunchy baked beans with slivers of pork so string dry you couldn't chew them.

Isabella was in charge of the cabin we were staying at. It

belonged to Adam Zebbs, she told us, a man who had run the underground and built this cabin last fall. Though he was gone now, he'd return by spring. Until then, it was ours to live in free as long as we kept it clean and neat. We had to promise not to use the one china plate with roses painted on it, as it belonged to Adam's wife.

"I'll be comin' by to tidy up for Adam," Isabella told us.

Levi smiled. "Adam sure is a fine builder. And the whole cabin is shinin' from your cleanin'. Never been in such a neat home. We gonna keep it this way for Adam."

He stood a long while at the door looking after Isabella when she walked off. A whole chicken leg disappeared in my mouth before he sat down to dinner.

* * *

Thought when I first came to Buxton that the days could not get any colder. But they did. Short dark winter days. Bitter long nights when the wind howled and we huddled in our warm feather beds. You could not stop still long if you were outside, that February. Best to keep moving. So we were always busy indoors or outdoors while the ground in the new world was sleeping beneath all that snow.

It never stopped Levi though. On those grey days he headed over to look at land to buy, all in fifty-acre parcels, with Will. They counted the trees and studied the way light fell across each plot. All they talked about come evening was buying land soon so they could clear some of it for spring planting.

On winter mornings, I was careful to give myself a good scrubbing at the wash basin, although it made me shivering cold. I even dunked my whole head and scrubbed so hard there was almost nothing left of my scalp. But Levi pointed to my hair flying every which way, so I slapped the hairs flat with

147

a wet hand to make them behave. Got my soles nailed on tight again. I stared at the clean blue shirt and pants Isabella said she had left in my room. I had never worn such fine things before. Would I dare wear them? Not yet, I decided.

When I was done, Levi whistled at the sight of the new me. "Is that you, Sol?"

The next few weeks fell into a pattern. Sundays, church came first. Reverend King's sermons so bold and fiery, you had to sit bolt upright. Nobody budged. We kept our eyes straight on the bonfire that was him. Weekdays, Levi was already gone by the time I got up. He found a job working at the railroad, cutting ties for seven cents each like most of the men, so they could pay for their farms.

One day Levi surprised me. "Just bought fifty acres, three miles north of town. This land is gonna be all ours in a few years," he said. "I still got what you earned. Haven't touched it yet. You might need it some day."

In the late afternoon, he'd go out to the land to chop down trees, stack wood to sell, and plan where to build his cabin and where to plant. I joined him after school until deep dark. Sure felt like we were back in Little Africa working side by side.

* * *

More winter days passed at the Buxton Mission School. Whenever I stepped into the school, it was full of surprises and learning. Each eye unblinking. All chins up. Our bodies listening still. My body leaned in toward Mister Dillon, while the others sat straight-backed. Beulah studied his every syllable. His words buzzed around in my head, circling and prying each hidden corner. Seemed to me we were like bees fixed on gathering the pollen dusted all over his words.

One morning, I stared around the classroom and watched

how each pencil moved in time with his dictation just like thoughts passing from mind to mind. For the first time, I wanted to see those words written down on my very own slate. I didn't pay attention because I had to or else, like back in slavery or in Mister Wellington's presence. I listened because I wanted to.

Maybe it was his voice. It sounded deep and loud, shooting like bullets from his belly He was fond of hearing our voices too, especially poetry. I could recite a poem along with the rest once I heard it said a few times. Poems got branded in my mind along with prayers like the 23rd Psalm: *Yea, though I walk through the valley of the shadow of death, I will fear no evil: For thou art with me.* Whatever anyone had ever *told* me, I remembered. Folks always said I was a good listener. I didn't need to be told anything twice. But written words swam before my eyes like specks of dirt on the page.

Emanuel fingered the words in the reader three of us shared and said them aloud at the same time. Beulah, on his other side, muttered them beneath her breath. But I was mute. The spoken word seemed to have no connection to those strange symbols on the page.

What I enjoyed most was studying the schoolmaster. I began to watch him while the others were pondering their books. He noticed small things: the lace patterns of snowflakes; the accent of a syllable; even my blue shirt. That was the day I was wearing Isabella's sweet-smelling shirt and new jeans for the first time.

He spun around soon as he saw me. "Today you are shining, Solomon!"

The next week, he surprised me again. Beulah appeared in a gingham dress with a wide skirt that had a ribbon of black around its hem that she said was velvet. She twirled around in the cloakroom, showing it to some girls. I could hear Zemenia, the prettiest girl of all, admiring it with "Ohh!" Then down the aisle Beulah swayed, touching desks on either side with the tip of her skirt.

"Why, Beulah, you look so fine in that dress," the schoolmaster said. "It makes you look like a young lady going to a dance."

Beulah swished her skirts as she sat down. A big smile lit her face. She no longer looked like the haunted girl I met in that lean-to. To me, she gave her first word since slavery. But that day, she gave her first smile to Mister Dillon.

* * *

Sometimes I drifted. I must admit that. Especially when the older students were working silently or taking a test and Emanuel could not tutor us. But I would rather be chopping trees in the woods instead. It's a job that sure warms you through and through. I was just like Levi, who had to be outside working, not sitting still all day long. I wondered what time it was and if we would be let out of school soon. So I looked out to study the light.

That was the first time I saw him.

I thought I was seeing things. It was dusk, the time of day when your eyes play tricks on you. From the schoolhouse window, I was staring at the cemetery right between the schoolhouse and the road when something moved out there. It stood still a long while. Then I thought it moved on again. *Could a ghost have got loose from its grave?* I wondered.

The shivering began in my neck, shooting up and down my back, setting all my skin tingling. I'd seen my fill of ghosts already; I didn't imagine they'd be living in Buxton too. I never stopped in that cemetery, but ran around it to get where I was going. It held the bodies of the slaves who had crossed over and died. We were ordered not to run or play on their graves. I'd never go near such a place. I had promised Grannie that, long ago.

The next afternoon was grey when I looked out. But it was still light enough to see a shadow by a tombstone. Someone was walking between the tombstones and wooden crosses and lingering at each one. The figure kind of rocked back and forth like it was praying. So cold out there I couldn't imagine anyone wanted to stay. A strange man was trudging among the dead out there, not minding spirits or the cold. What called him there, all alone? Maybe he was getting ready to join the ghosts. Or maybe he was already one of them.

"You saw it — someone? — in the cemetery this afternoon?" I asked Emanuel after school let out.

"That's Old Ezekiel. He's an elder, the oldest one living here. They say he knows everything about slavery and which people came to Canada."

"How does he know?"

Emanuel shrugged. "Guess you got to be old to remember everything. They say if you want to know about anybody, where they are, if they are living or dead, he's the one who'll know."

Such a wondering took hold of me. Books filled this schoolhouse. But no book held what my heart wished to know. Maybe one who had lived so long and seen so much could help me find the ones I had lost.

Chapter 25
KEEPER OF THE STORIES

Late February 1858

THE EVENING BELLS RANG. Our dinner basket was set on the table, waiting.

Isabella looked up from gathering our work clothes into a bundle for washing. "Listen! May they be free soon! May Adam bring them home."

"Who you speakin' about, Miss?" I asked her.

"Adam built this house here for his wife and three children livin' on a Kentucky farm, still in slavery. That's where he went last fall, to bring 'em back."

I gasped. "You mean Adam can go back and it'll be all right?"

"Reverend King arranged for Adam's safe passage to abolitionists in Ohio. It's very dangerous, but they planned to send him South when the time was right. Been no word about him yet."

"He must be a brave man," I said. "I hope he finds them soon."

She smiled at me. "Can't wait to hear those bells ring for Adam's family when he brings them home."

Levi walked in then, stomping his boots in the doorway. "Seems I always come home just when the evenin' bells ring. Always makin' me think of those we left behind. Like my pa Enos, and Jacob too. May God set them free!"

Why did Levi have to say that? I didn't need any reminder.

Didn't Grandpa's black boots sit underneath my bed? There seemed no way to find out if Grandpa still lived and had got across. Maybe I'd never know. Adam had more courage than most — he could not wait for his family, but went back to save them. That's what I'd like to do. Maybe I could find out about someone else, though — my pa, and if he ever got free. All I had to know was if he was alive and where, and I'd run right to him. Nothing would stop me. So I promised myself the first chance I got, I'd speak to Old Ezekiel. He'd been living so close to the dead and forgotten ones, he surely would understand me.

The next day was bitter cold with wind blowing snow all around so that it stung your face like flying pine needles. I ran out after the school day was done and stood in the field. Old Ezekiel trudged past, silent and slow, so close I could have tugged on his coat. He was wrapped up against the cold, so I could not see his face. I stared after him. Surely someone so old knew most everything. Like whether folks were alive or . . . or . . . dead. That terrible thought stopped my feet from running after him. Questions rose up inside me like hornets out of their spring nest. But I couldn't get the words from my head to my lips to ask him.

If you listen close, you could help me. The words were there inside me, waiting, but I couldn't let them out.

Then I saw where the elder was headed — into the middle of the cemetery. Into the darkest shadows. He was surely going to speak to the dead. He'd know if someone I loved was already a ghost. Better I heard nothing than to hear that. I ran off quick the other way. Told myself that Levi was waiting for me anyway.

He'd cleared over half an acre already. Some wood he sold for firewood to shops in town. The widest oaks he cut down on his day off, and left them out to dry. They would be finished at the mill. I set to work beside him now as he sang in a loud voice and chopped down tree limbs for firewood beside the light of our campfire. Even after a full day's work for the railroad, Levi got busy working as soon as he stepped into his own woods. From across the road where he had bought his own land, Will joined us, prying the smallest stumps from the ground with his horse. Most stumps would not budge yet, so we left them there to rot. They'd be ready to pull up eventually.

On Saturdays, Levi always stopped work early. Before dusk, he hurried home and washed. He actually pressed a comb through his hair and changed into clean pants, whistling. Nobody had to tell me he was waiting on Isabella. I had never noticed grown women before. Levi said Isabella was just a little younger than him, living with her parents, who had crossed over when she was my age. Every time she called, Levi lit up like he was standing in the light of a hundred candles. She walked in a cloud of sweet smells. Maybe it was the soap from all her washing or the baking smell of applesauce that lingered about her clothes. She always brought something with her. A stew of pork and potatoes. Corn pones or buttermilk biscuits. Wild raspberry preserves. Roasted turkey. And fresh laundry too.

One evening when I stepped into the cabin, it seemed to glow. That told me Isabella was around. Levi was struck dumb in her presence as usual. Hard to believe him having nothing to say. He followed her with his eyes as she dusted the cabin. But somehow, his mouth wasn't working. He was in a spell.

Isabella worked quietly, but every so often she looked my way and smiled. I could feel her studying me just like I studied the schoolmaster. She passed by as she mopped, and slipped an apple into my pocket. Then she asked where I came from and how we survived on the underground road. She wondered why I was all alone. So many questions she had. Nobody had ever asked them of me before.

"Everybody who ran here like you, left somebody behind," she murmured.

Words exploded out of me — all the words I'd been waiting to tell. I told her what happened to my family and that all I thought about was where my pa and grandpa were.

She paused to listen to my every word. "You got to speak to Old Ezekiel," she told me. "If anyone knows about your pa, he's the one. Why don't you go to him?"

She set her large brown eyes upon me, waiting for an answer. But I could say nothing then. The words rose up and swelled in a big lump in my throat and I had to turn away.

* * *

By the end of February, I had made friends with some boys like David, yet I did not speak to Zemenia, as I wanted to. She was Beulah's best friend now and since they were always together, I trailed right beside them. I knew more letters now. The names of the Great Lakes in Canada, and all the continents of the world, I knew by memory. I could even draw the exact shape of Lake Erie, whose shoreline we had once followed to get here. But when it came to tests where I had to write those same answers down, I could only guess at their spellings. I did not pass one test. Something stood between me and learning. If only I could confess to somebody how all the words jammed up inside and mixed together in such a tangle, my hands could not set them down clearly. Mister Dillon was the one to confess to, but the very thought made me quiver. I didn't want him to think me worthless.

How could I tell the schoolmaster I always hid a big piece of my mind deep inside my heart? Wouldn't show it to nobody but Grandpa. I was most like an ostrich with its head stuck in the ground. Been like that so long, how could I get free now? It'd been easy to give up on Mister Wellington. He didn't care a half-penny about me. But with the new schoolmaster, how I wished with all my might I wasn't so stupid. Mister Dillon tapped his way inside me like a bold woodpecker poking into a dead tree, looking at me with his wide eyes burning, asking questions of me all the time.

It was me who wanted to ask questions of *him*. And to tell him all about my pa and my grandpa. Maybe he'd know a way to get to them. If I could find them both again, I could learn. If my family lived beside me, I could grow roots like I had begun to do in Little Africa. Every time Mr. Dillon was near, words leaped inside me, though not one fell from my lips. Over a hundred children sat in that classroom and no one spoke to the schoolmaster unless called upon. So I waited and waited while the February days grew a little longer.

Soon there was a space of light opening between the end of the school day and the beginning of dark. Late one afternoon, Old Ezekiel appeared by the edge of the cemetery at such a time. If I couldn't go to Mister Dillon, this was my only chance to ask for help. If I didn't do it now, I'd be lost like Pa and Grandpa.

Into that dusk, I walked.

Go. Go before he gets into the back of the cemetery where the shadows are darkest, I told myself. I ran up to him and tugged on his arm and he stopped. Slowly he turned my way and studied me like you do a tree, a living thing that can't talk back. His eyes were slits of bright suns upon me. But he did not speak.

156

I stepped back and held still. You don't ever see such a man often. So old, with a face like warped tree roots as if he lived underground, and a blue shine to his skin like indigo dye. He stood with a blanket over his shoulders in the middle of the snow. Looking at him, I thought I was on the underground again, back in some dream.

"What . . . what do you do here?" I asked him.

His voice creaked wide open, rusty and deep, like he hadn't used it in a long while. "Rememberin'. Makin' records of all those who have gone . . . in case anyone comes lookin' for 'em."

I gulped. Maybe my pa was already here in this cold ground. I had to find out. "I heard . . . you know about all the families who ran north."

"I am the keeper of the stories," the elder said. "No one's gonna remember what we went through to get here if someone doesn't hold them tight."

"But where do you keep the stories? They say you can't read or write."

Such a deep rumble in Old Ezekiel's chest. Couldn't tell if he was laughing or coughing.

"Stories hit here first." He smacked his heart. "Then they go up to my mind. Nobody's got the key but me. You give me a name, and I tell you their story. First, I sit with the sound of their name until it hums through me and finds the key to open all the words."

My whole body was burning. I'd been waiting for this moment.

"Isam!" The word popped out of hiding. "From the Tiller plantation in Georgia. He ran almost six years ago in the springtime."

Then Old Ezekiel asked what more I knew about my pa,

anything to help him remember. I was only six when he left, so there wasn't much to tell. Whenever anyone recalled my pa, they only said, "Oh, he's one who took the underground." Not what he looked like or if anyone heard from him. You don't hear from anyone who took the underground. That's the rule. If they were living, they were up in the northern states, or in Canada, so they were free. But the other reason is worse — maybe they got caught, or died, and never made it to Canada. Maybe they never crossed over but were living in fear in the North, hoping nobody claimed them. You might never know what happened to them.

But then I remembered what I thought I had forgotten: the almond shape of his eyes; and his hand in my hair, tickling light, until I fell asleep.

When I told him these things, Old Ezekiel closed his eyes. His head nodded up and down like he was listening to a tune from somewhere far off. His lips mumbled words I couldn't understand, like he was speaking a spell. He seemed to forget anyone was standing there beside him.

"Come back later," I finally heard him say. "Let your story sit inside me a while."

I nodded and ran off, not daring to ask right off what I'd been most worried about. All the while I prayed he had not already found Pa lying in that cold cemetery ground.

Chapter 26
LETTERS IN MY MIND

March 1858

MURMURING. WORDS CHANTED OVER AND OVER. Low and spoken softly.

We woke to find the cabin surrounded. A ring of Buxton folks stood outside in the cold grey dawn, praying. Some held hands. Others carried candles. Someone cried out.

"The evening and dawn bells gonna ring for Adam now. May God protect him and help him live through this," Isabella announced.

Levi ran out. "What's happened?"

Jenny, our neighbour from down the road, moaned. "Reverend King got a letter this morning. Adam was captured in the South, sent back to his master and whipped hard. Don't know if he's gonna survive. Or what will happen now. Hope they don't harm his children or wife."

"We told Adam not to cross back over," Chloe cried. "Now we fear what's gonna happen to him. Down there, in that land, no one's gonna save a runaway."

Then the dawn bells tolled, loud and heavy in our ears. *Remember us,* they said.

"What will happen to his place?" Levi asked Isabella.

"Adam paid up for two years. He planned on settling here with his family. Reverend King said he will honour that and await his return to Buxton."

"May God free him and his family!" someone shouted.

159

I remembered the china plate then. It sat alone and unused on a shelf. Adam's wife had never seen it or even imagined she could own one. She might never come now.

I'd never go back to the United States or pass close to its border. Danger was there. Freedom was here. The whole town of Buxton was hidden safe inside these woods.

I ran off as soon as I bolted my breakfast down, so I wouldn't be late for school. It was a place of signs and wonders, and each day I wanted to see what would happen next.

* * *

The Queen's English was hard enough to pronounce, and worse yet to write down, and now the other students seemed to be speaking in tongues. That very morning, Bessie stood up in front of the whole class and spouted a whole list of words that stretched her lips out flat. I was worried she was having a fit. These odd-sounding words I had heard before but paid no attention to them. No one had gotten up and dropped a whole string of them like that. All the words were meaningless, but I did catch one and thought I heard her say, *"Aud-io!"* None of the words were sweet sounding, but dull and hard. Yet Mister Dillon tapped his yardstick in time with her words as if they were music. I do believe he smiled. Then he pointed to the class, beating that stick on one of the desks and all repeated the words except Beulah and me.

"It's Latin," David whispered.

He was a tall white boy who said his pa sent him to Buxton's school because it was the best one around, better than the all-white schools in the district.

"Who's Latin?"

"Latin's a *language*. So old nobody speaks it anymore except us. You can learn any other language once you know Latin.

Even helps with English. What Bessie was saying was verbs like *audio,* meaning *I hear.*"

Of course, I didn't believe him.

Then the schoolmaster pointed to a sign and Emanuel read it aloud: *Cogito ergo sum.*

"This Latin motto tells us something remarkable about our mind. Can anyone translate it?"

Bessie shot up her hand like a salute. "I think. Therefore I am!"

He led us in a chant next that David said was about a house: "*domus, domus; domus, domorum; domu, domibus . . .*"

In those Latin lessons, I began to stare out the window looking for Old Ezekiel. He usually appeared in the afternoon, but sometimes he'd walk in the mornings, then disappear for days. Why hadn't he looked for me yet? Maybe he knew something about my pa and didn't want to tell me. I thought about the nightmare that had come again last night. I'd been dreaming it over and over for years. . . . *I am resting in our cabin when men rush in. Blood on my hands. Blood on the floor. A man falling down. And the insides of me falling with him . . .*

I was sure now that it was not a dream after all. Something happened that changed everything that long ago day, but I could not remember what it was.

After the Arithmetic lesson, which I paid no attention to, Emanuel kept jabbing me with his elbow to make me do my sums. But I was drifting back and back. Pictures came to me. I tried not to look but the memories were like a big box. Once you opened it, you must peek inside . . . How Grandpa had already waved goodbye to me forever and I never knew at the time. That's how I stupid I was. That's why he never turned around — he didn't want me to guess. If I'd seen his sad face,

I'd never have left him. If only I'd stayed, we'd be together now . . . I banged my leg with my fist for letting him go. Until Emanuel hissed that he had enough and was ready to raise his hand and tell the schoolmaster everything if I didn't do my work that instant.

"Listen to me, Solomon! Do you hear me?"

"I *audio* you!" I muttered.

Emanuel's head jerked and his eyes lit up. "That's wonderful, Solomon. You remembered just by listening. Well done. *Maximus in minimis!*"

"Hmm?"

"It means 'great in little things.'"

I didn't know whether he was insulting me or saying something nice.

Emanuel was actually grinning and he and I chuckled all through Arithmetic, me counting on my fingers underneath the desk just like Beulah. I got all the sums correct. He spared me from Division that day, which I could not do at all.

But soon the letters spun in my head like it was a mixing bowl. That was because in that classroom they spoke Greek too. Maybe they were practising it all along and I hadn't really paid much attention until that moment. It sounded very odd, almost as bad as Latin. David swore it was another old language I was hearing. When they spoke it, I set my elbows on the desk and my chin in my hands. Nobody guessed I was jamming my fingers tight in my ears. Latin got stirred up with the Queen's English and I soon forgot all the names of the continents. My spelling was so bad that Emanuel said I could not hand in my exercise book looking that way. So he made me rewrite it over and over again until I got it right.

* * *

162

One March afternoon, I was ready to plop my head down on the desk when a shadow shifted outside at the edge of the snowy field. Old Ezekiel was standing very still, facing the schoolhouse, looking straight at its windows. Then he moved on, into the paths through the cemetery. When the school bell finally rang, my feet were the first out the door.

Old Ezekiel was waiting for me in front of a thin grey tombstone. His hand reached out to touch it. When he saw me beside him, his head lifted and he stared right at me. A low fire burned in his eyes like ash in a fireplace at the end of the evening. There was no choice but to stand still and listen, holding my breath.

"Isam from the Tiller plantation. I do remember such a man," Old Ezekiel said. "Wanted to get as far away from slavery as he could. Be deep in the woods, way up north around Owen Sound maybe, where many of our folk settled. Wanted to be like the trees, he said, safe and free."

With those words, I jumped. I knew this was my very own pa because I felt the same way inside. He was just like me, running to the trees. He was not buried in this cold ground. He was alive in Canada! I had to find him. I was ready to walk all the way north that very minute. So I asked Old Ezekiel for directions.

"Can't go there now," he told me when I asked that. "Cold up there, and the snow so high it'd bury you. You know how far it is? A month's walk or more. Wait on the summer, when the goin' will be easy."

"Is there no way to get to him now?"

"I only got letters in my mind. If I could read and write like you young ones, I'd write him. But it's too late for me to learn. Think you can do it?"

I never expected this question from Old Ezekiel. Not this. Hoped he'd set me on the road and tell me the way to Pa. Such a trembling down the middle of me. I took off running, heading for the woods at the back of the cemetery. Maybe if I got real quiet, I'd hear my pa's voice telling me what to do. I couldn't wait until summer. He'd been up north six years. No telling where he'd go from there.

Feet pounding, legs flying, I made my mind flat and empty. I fell into a rhythm that hypnotized me. That's how I learned to listen deep. Each time I pressed one foot down, a word popped up. Then another. Seemed like a poem spoke right out of me.

Sometimes you must do hard things to get what you want.
Things that make you tremble and that you fear you cannot do.
Do them. You'll get yourself free.

But, what if I couldn't?

Chapter 27
THE LONG ROAD NORTH

Late March – Early April 1858

I RAN STRAIGHT TO LEVI to tell him the news. And my plan for him and me to head north right away. On foot. Like we'd travelled the underground. I knew Levi didn't always agree with me before, like when we were in Port Dover and Little Africa where I wanted to stay. But I'd grown plenty since then. We had learned to work together as a team. I did everything he said and laboured every single day at his side. Just one little thing I was asking of him right then.

But when I asked him, Levi never paused in his task of loading a wagon with firewood to sell.

"You and I have travelled a thousand miles to get to a safe place where we could live a good life, Solomon," he said. "I'm not steppin' foot outside Buxton and neither are you."

"But Pa is alive! And he's not so far away. He might not stay in one place forever. I got to get to him soon."

"Not now. It'd be dangerous to go farther north this time of year. Nobody would do such a thing — not even the strongest man around would take such a journey right now. Those roads up there are nothin' but bogs in the springtime. Snowstorms could come at any time too."

I stared at Levi. He *was* the tallest and strongest man in Buxton and he was not willing to go. He and I did not understand one another. We never had. I turned away and jammed my lips together.

165

Levi's words trailed behind me. "You are here doin' the best thing for now — gettin' schooled like your grandpa wanted."

If Levi would not go, I still had to. Pa was alive and he did not even know I was here in this country. I had to tell him. Soon.

A secret plan grew like a wild weed. The next day, I started asking questions of the settlers about the way to Owen Sound or anywhere near there — which road was quickest and how to find signposts along the route to guide you. Most had never gone so far north. The men shook their heads about travelling so far at winter's end.

"What you want to go up there for?" Mr. Sims asked. "No better spot than right here. It's all wilderness up there. Bears and cold. No easy plantin' like we got here either."

"The rails go as far as Collingwood, up in Simcoe County," said another settler. "That'd be the fastest way to reach it. But you need money to do that. And time off work. Not many of us could go."

I never said a word about why I wanted to go.

All that night, I stayed awake, seeing the snowy roads up north. I had to go. Even if I didn't know how to get there. The following day at school, I looked around the classroom to see if there was anybody strong enough to go with me up north. There was nobody. Beulah might have said yes — she knew what it was like to miss a father. But she was too young.

Beside me, Emanuel's pen scratched away. He was the oldest student in the room; maybe he would not need permission for a trip. He was working on an essay to a college in Toronto that he wished to learn at come fall. His pen flowed over the paper without stop. He did it so easy, there was no pause between what he thought and what he wrote down. I took

166

a deep breath and whispered my plans to him.

Emanuel's pen stopped. His eyes shifted my way and he immediately began to scold me.

"I can't go there! My parents would never allow it. And you can't go on your own! Be smart, Solomon. Why can't you write to your father instead? Let the letter travel the miles to find him, like Old Ezekiel told you."

Twice I'd been told and still couldn't imagine how I'd do it. I broke loose of the schoolhouse that afternoon like a wild cat. Each and every stone on my path, I kicked sky high. In the distance, somebody was yelling but I paid no mind. Then I heard my name.

"Wait up, Solomon!"

Levi was running along the path from Reverend King's house. He came to a halt right beside me. "You didn't sleep last night," he said. "Neither did I. All night long, I was figurin' a way to find your pa. I just spoke to Mr. King. Know what he's doin' right now?"

The front window at Mr. King's house was lamp lit.

"Reverend King knows somebody in Owen Sound. He's sittin' down to write him a letter askin' if anyone's seen your pa."

"He's gonna write a letter for me?"

Levi nodded. "Folks said he'd help out. And so he is. It'll go there by mail first thing tomorrow mornin'!"

My feet jumped so high, my cap hit an oak branch high above my head.

"C'mon!" laughed Levi. "Big happenings tomorrow. Gotta get ready for 'em. Let's run."

The two of us ran up Centre Road, my mouth open wide the whole way, screaming and filling with cold, spring air.

* * *

The very next day, we were too busy to think much. Everything changed that Friday. Though I'd heard about it, I never saw it happen with my own eyes. One day, nothing's there but air, they say. Next day, a cabin stands in that spot. Seemed like magic. Until you saw them work.

Twelve men showed up before dawn on the muddy road by Levi's new land. A day was all they needed, the work gang said. All around them were boards laid out this way and that on the ground, marking the measurements of the cabin. Rough hewn logs from Levi's woods set aside for the hard outside walls. Smooth oak planks from Buxton's sawmill for the floors. Bricks for the chimney. The boss shouted orders and the twelve men worked as one man lifting the logs. I had to go to school by then.

It was hard to sit still inside and wait. Not one thing did I learn that day. Soon as the bell rang, I ran the three miles north to the land, with Zemenia, who was our back neighbour now, trying to keep up with my flying heels.

I couldn't believe my eyes when we finally got to Levi's. Seven hours had passed and now our cabin stood up straight. Lots of banging and hammering inside, so we couldn't go in. The chimney was being raised along with walls separating the front room from the bedrooms. Levi was building a picket fence. Other men were finishing a small barn behind the cabin. I was soon ordered to pick up the baby chicks from Zemenia's barn and bring the horse too. Levi had sold enough wood to the sawmill to make extra money to buy such things.

"You must keep the chicks warm," Zemenia told me. "If you take care of them, they'll follow you like you are their family."

She handed some chicks to me, slipping them inside my shirt, next to my bare skin, for the trip back. She carried some in a handkerchief. The chicks were fuzzy yellow and bright-eyed and wiggled all the way. I wrapped the horse's rope around my waist as we crossed the field to Levi's. We led the horse into the new barn and set the chicks down in straw. Inside, the horse's breath puffed clouds into the cold spring air.

Zemenia petted the chicks, which ran in circles, chirping and examining their new home, then back to her for another touch. They stuck their beaks inside her pockets, searching for food, and pecked grain out of her open hands. Soon they fell asleep in a heap at her feet.

I'd never been so close up to Zemenia before. She was the same age as me and had so much hair that it kept falling into her eyes. It was a black so deep and dark it matched her eyes. I sure wanted to touch its waves, but didn't dare.

The next week we packed our belongings and left Adam's house. We were careful to sweep and leave it just as we found it. Isabella said a family of new arrivals was already waiting to live there. I figured that meant there was still no word from Adam. I gave one last look to the china plate and said a prayer for Adam and his family.

* * *

We spent all our spare time building beds, a table and chairs; then we cleared a garden space behind the cabin. One Sunday morning, Reverend King was shaking folks' hands after church services. He stood tall and smiling in the doorway of the church as we all left. But when he saw Levi and me coming, his smile disappeared. He stopped us, set his hand upon my shoulder, and led us to one side, away from all the chattering churchgoers.

"I received a letter from Father Thomas Henry Miller in Owen Sound," he said.

The two of us stood there silently. Finally he asked if we'd like to hear the answer. We both nodded. I leaned back, right into Levi's hard chest.

"Isam Tiller passed through a year ago. He's gone now," he read from the letter in his hands. *"We'll ask in Collingwood, and other towns in Grey County, to see if anyone knows of him."* Mr. King did not let go of me. Neither did Levi. If they hadn't been there, I'd have fallen.

I heard Mr. King's deep voice say, "We'll wait for better news, Solomon. Someone is sure to have heard of your pa. Don't lose heart."

Our walk home was slow. Reverend King was the most important man in the whole of Buxton. But his letter had not travelled into Pa's hands like I'd hoped.

How could I ever find him now?

Chapter 28
NOSCE TE IPSUM

IN MY DREAMS THAT SAME MARCH NIGHT, *a man wandered. He roamed from place to place and did not settle. Nobody knew his name. Nobody could keep up with him. He was a stranger. An outcast. He had lost his only home. All he had was memories and he did not want them either. His hair was streaked with grey. He was walking toward a field of wooden crosses and he did not stop.*

"PA! WHERE ARE YOU?"

In the grey, between the tombstones, the man stopped. Had he heard me? . . .

Hands grabbed my shoulders and shook hard. "Wake up, Sol! You're safe in Buxton. You've had a bad dream, that's all. You woke me up with all your screamin'." It was Levi. He was sitting right beside me.

My body was so tired, like it had no sleep at all, like I was back roaming the underground road.

"Nightmares again?" he asked.

"Pa! I saw my pa . . . near a cemetery, all alone."

Levi sighed. Last night, neither of us spoke about the letter that had not found Pa. Levi got up and paced around my bed a few times, then finally sat down again.

"When the days turn warmer and our plants are growin', you and me will go up to some of the towns farther north. I promise you we'll find your pa, just like we found Buxton,

171

Sol. Can you wait just a while longer? 'Til summer?"

I swallowed hard. Levi and I had been through everything together and it was just now that he'd finally noticed me.

I shook my head slowly. "I got to do somethin' right now."

"Don't you do anythin' foolish, Sol. Let me know your plans."

"All right," I said. "When I know, I'll tell you."

Into that cool, grey morning I ran hard without breakfast all the way to school. It was much too early for it to open. Its doors were shut. But I felt sure I had to be there. Then I remembered the man in my dreams and how he was headed toward the tombstones in the cemetery. Over there, past the school, between the tombstones along the road, a shadow shifted. So thin and dark, I wasn't sure it was there. Then it turned. Old Ezekiel appeared out of nowhere. Like the grey fog was part of him, the weight of all the names he carried, all the old stories that had travelled miles and years from far-off Africa, resting inside him. My feet started running toward him.

"Somethin' happen?" he asked right off.

"Reverend King sent a letter. Got the answer yesterday. My pa's gone off. They say he might be . . . be anywhere, maybe in Collingwood, maybe somewhere else in Grey County. They promised to send out word to look for him."

Old Ezekiel turned so slowly away from me that I could hear his bones creaking and cracking like he was an old tree. Then I realized what he was doing. He was facing toward Grey County. Then he turned farther away, northeast, toward where they say Collingwood is, on the edge of Georgian Bay.

Minutes passed. It grew lighter. I shivered in the cold.

Old Ezekiel finally began to turn my way. "Give me your hands," he said.

I put them forward. He placed them in his wide, open palms and studied them.

"These hands know your pa. There's somethin' only these hands of yours can do, son. You must write the letter *yourself* and mail it to this place — Collingwood. Then you will find Isam Tiller. You alone have the power to find him."

I couldn't say one word. I couldn't even breathe. All I could do was stare at Old Ezekiel until all the voices started calling and yelling and the children arrived for school. I ran off when the bell rang.

Soon as I saw Emanuel I ran up to him and tugged on his sleeve. "Remember what you said about my writing a letter to my pa? You seen my letters? Even you can't read 'em. It'll take me years to do it. Unless . . . unless you write it for me. Would you?"

Emanuel pursed his lips together. "Certainly I could write the letter *for* you. But don't you want to write it *yourself*? You are so close to learning. You know most letters. All you have to do is string them together into words. I'll help. Don't you want the words to come from you to your own father?"

What he and Old Ezekiel both said was what I always wanted — for the words to ring out of me clear and true as the Liberty Bell. Such words would have the power to find what I was searching for, like an arrow winging to a target.

But how could I call them out of hiding?

* * *

Each school-day morning afterwards, I awoke early in our new cabin. I wanted to be wide awake for the day's lessons. If I couldn't go up north yet, I could try learning, at least until summer, when Levi said he'd take me there. Maybe today would be the day that I would make a leap and write easy. I waited for Zemenia to cross the fields and join Beulah and me for the three-mile walk to the Mission School. Will and Beulah's cabin was so nearby, she and I could call one other to come over from across the road.

"You gonna be in the recitin' contest?" Zemenia asked me first thing.

Beulah said. "Bet you could win!"

Between the two of them, they insisted I memorize one of Mister Dillon's favourite poems, William Blake's "The Tyger." What I needed to do was write, but since neither of them knew how either, other than a few words, I went along with what they wanted. As we skipped back and forth to school, I recited the lines aloud. Soon I could say the poem in my sleep. On the day of the contest, several students recited poems, each sounding perfect and lovely. But David stumbled over a word and Moses didn't speak loud enough. Next it was Bessie's turn. She recited a passage from Homer and the schoolmaster's eyes were set upon her the whole while like a magnet.

Then it was my turn. I stood in the front of the classroom for the very first time. But my lips did not move. My mind was suddenly blank. The bright faces of the students looked on. How I wished they were my brothers and sisters. They were fortunate; they had a father or mother living in Buxton. If only my own pa was here, I knew for sure my mind would be clear to learn. But though he lived in the same country as me, I was no closer to seeing him now than those years I'd lived on the plantation without him. No one in my family even knew where I was. I was all alone.

Such a pang shot through me. *Where are you, Pa? Why can't I see you?*

He was small like Grandpa. But I couldn't recall his face anymore. Not clear, anyway. It seemed so long ago he was with me. I tried calling up Grandpa's face next. It was fading away too. I couldn't hold on to either one.

My body turned all by itself, and before I knew it I was running out of the schoolhouse, tears dripping, out to the first place that would hide me, between the oak tree and the outhouse. Leaning against the wall, I let loose a wall of tears, tears I had never let out, all those tears that once jammed inside me like a frozen river. When I was done, I knew I would never cry again. Nothing left inside.

That's when the bell rang. The children would run out and ask all kinds of questions. So I squatted against the back of the outhouse. So much shouting and laughter flying around me and then all was quiet. I was getting ready to sneak home when I saw polished black leather boots facing my way — Mister Dillon's boots.

"Let me quit, sir!" I stood up, eyes on the ground, hands squeezed in fists in my pockets. "I'm not ever gonna catch up to 'em or even come close."

"Some of these students began school at five, Solomon," he told me. "They were born here in Canada. Like Emanuel. They are the fortunate. Those I push hard. Others have been here a few months and are just now starting to write. It takes time. Everyone must begin where they are. All my students learn to read and write, every single one."

"Sir, I don't mean to argue with you. But I can't be like them."

"Don't you think I know what it is like to come up from slavery? It's in the faces of the young and old around this settlement. Suffering. Leaning way back into oneself. But I also see men walking straight for the first time in their lives, children adding sums better than their parents, and Buxton's graduates attending medical school in Toronto. If you try, I will try even harder. I will help you, Solomon."

"And you, sir, how did you learn?"

"I was one of the fortunate. My parents were free and living in the North. Still, they couldn't find good schooling for my brother and me. So they moved to Buxton to better themselves."

That's why this man shone. He was born to a father already free, a father who wanted the best for him and guided him to it.

"You must love your father," I told him. "As I love mine. But I don't even know whether he still lives."

Mister Dillon's eyes set on me like light beams.

I looked right into them. "Help me find him, sir."

And then I told him everything. The words heaved right out of me. All about Old Ezekiel saying that my father had gone up north somewhere. How Mr. King's letter was answered. And how I couldn't wait any longer to find Pa. And Old Ezekiel saying I must be the one to write to Pa. Even how I could not learn at all.

"There is a way to find your father. I'll help if you want to learn. Once you know your alphabet, you can write him a letter. It could be in his hands not long after."

Could letters I wrote really have the power to search for my pa when all the walking and rambling across this big country had not done so yet? My heart was racing ahead without me, wanting to know more.

I'd wanted to run up north; I'd wanted someone to go with me; I'd wanted Emanuel to write the letter. But now it was just me who had to do the hardest thing there was — to write.

Suddenly my chest opened wide and my whole body glowed. I couldn't help but smile. I wanted to learn everything then. I couldn't wait any longer. This time, I wouldn't be alone. Mister Dillon would help me. He'd know a way to free my mind so my hands would know what to do.

"S. O. L. O. M. O. N." I recited the letters to him straight away.

Mister Dillon laughed then. "Oh, but there are more letters than that. And you will learn them soon. You don't seem to care for Latin, but sometimes it says things best. *Nosce te ipsum* means *Know thyself*. And you do, Solomon. You know what you want. You've always known. Now you just have to trust what is in your heart."

That was the beginning of more schooling. Levi had to wait an extra hour each school-day afternoon for me to do chores. He teased me plenty about sticking my own foot in my mouth by asking Mister Dillon for help.

I didn't complain. I stayed with Beulah and some others, all the new ones, in a small circle with the schoolmaster, who sat down right in our midst. Before he let us go, we each had to write a new word we'd learned that day.

Dear Pa, I wrote that first day. I recited those words as I fell asleep each night. Just two words is all I wrote — the first words I wrote with all my heart.

Chapter 29
BUSY WITH WORDS

Late April – Late May 1858

NOBODY EVER SAW ME BEFORE. I wouldn't let them. Most of my life as a slave, I had to hide every little bit of what I was thinking. I was my own shadow. But from the very first day Mister Dillon looked at me, when I saw all the dirt covering me, I wanted to look as gleaming as him.

Odd how a boy could be so different depending on who he was with. Only one person ever really saw me, and that was Grandpa. Whenever Master Tiller looked through me, waiting on me to grow so I could work harder and longer, I wanted to shrink. Levi shoved me along and kept looking straight ahead. But being pinned beneath Mister Dillon's gaze was breath-held awe, heart-thumping. I could suddenly see myself through his eyes, all I could be. Made me want to leap sky high to get there.

My own shaky fingers wrote the letter at last.

It took a whole week. Lots of fixings by the schoolmaster, but it came out clear and true one day. Emanuel and the schoolmaster had been right after all. I was close to learning and did not know it.

April 25, 1858

Dear Pa,

I write these words myself from Buxton. Old Ezekiel remembered you passed through here on your way north.

178

Is it true? Are you really living up there?

I pray these words find you wherever you may be. Please come find me.

Your son living in freedom,
Solomon

I leaped like a frog, then ran down to mail the letter at the post office. Mister Dillon had addressed it to the postmaster of Collingwood, a man he had heard would help out. None other than Buxton's postmaster himself would receive my letter, I decided. That way, it would have his touch to send it off. Buxton's postmaster was a heavy man who plopped down in his wooden chair like he never stood the whole day long. Just his hands moved, sorting letters. Finally he looked up and I placed my letter into his open hand.

"It'll leave first thing tomorrow mornin'," he said, reading the address. "Road's muddy to Chatham, so it might not go out on the train until the next day or so."

"That long, sir? When will it get to Collingwood?"

He shrugged. "Can't predict the weather. If there's a snowstorm, it may slow the trains goin' north."

He was right. Everywhere in Buxton, folks waited for the fields to dry out from snowmelt. Neighbours had given us corn and collard seeds, but we dared not risk planting them yet. Not even potatoes, advised Mr. Sims, whose last year's crop had rotted in the ground. Will and Levi kept clearing and ploughing, though they were stuck so often, seemed they spent most of their time freeing the plough. Skies were grey every day and then it rained hard. Out in the rain, you could see the men digging drainage ditches alongside the roads and fields, instead of planting.

* * *

At the Mission School, we were busy with words. One day, we practised for the next reciting contest. When it was my turn to try, Mr. Dillon allowed me to stand by my desk, where I recited looking straight at the blackboard. I didn't dare look at anyone: "Tyger! Tyger! Burning bright / in the forests of the night. / What immortal hand or eye / could frame thy fearful symmetry?" I was buzzing words like a bee in daisy petals. Words dripped out like honey at some "honeyfest" — the exact words of the poem. It made me chuckle that I had just made up a new word. I almost let loose a laugh at that one. Until Mister Dillon stopped in his strolling beside my desk and looked at my face.

"Is that *Solomon* smiling?" the schoolmaster asked.

"Well, um, just a little, sir."

Silence. He looked at my tidy desk and my polished boots and the penmanship I had practised with Emanuel. He nodded and walked on. "It certainly suits you to smile, young Solomon. Makes you look handsome."

Oh, the fluttering of girls' eyelashes at that one. And the tittering from the boys. Even Beulah turned my way, with her mouth open wide in the shape of an *O*. But the schoolmaster had reached the front of the classroom and was facing us now. The moment was over. He allowed us a little laugh now and then. I did not care if it was at my own expense. And the laugh stayed deep inside me, light as a bubble, lifting my chest that whole afternoon.

I complained to Beulah and Zemenia later that day at recess. "Girls come right up to me and start talking. But the boys stand back and don't say much."

Beulah laughed. "You don't know why?"

Zemenia just stared at me. She didn't say a word.

"Maybe I am too ugly with these ears stickin' up, and girls move close in to stare at 'em," I told them. "Tell me the truth. Is that what it is?"

Zemenia reached up to touch my ears but she couldn't find them. They were buried beneath a mess of hair.

"Nobody ever saw your ears," she said. "Those girls are too busy lookin' at your eyelashes — thick and long and curlin' on your cheek. And your big almond eyes. Easy to look at you. Besides, you're not full of mischief, like most boys tuggin' our braids."

She put her hand over her mouth and bit back her lips to hide her smile. Beulah grinned at us and skipped away.

* * *

As the weather warmed in the late May fields, there was a feeling in the fresh spring air of new beginnings. Poppies flared bright red in the flower beds in front of all the cabins. The birds found Buxton again, filling the air with chirping until dark and nesting in the lone oak near Levi's cabin. Geese returned too and were often Sunday's dinner. Isabella sewed white curtains and hung them in our new windows. Sunbright days dried the fields. One by one, seeds were dropped into the ground. Within weeks, you could see green sprouts all in a straight line: collards, mustard greens, turnips and cabbage. Levi fell asleep in his chair after dinner, a tired smile on his face.

Even Mister Dillon looked brand new. He wore a fancy black-and-grey striped suit with a vest and paced up and down the rows like his feet were on fire. He had visited the big city of Toronto recently. He gathered all the new students into a small group while the others worked. We sat open-mouthed while we heard about the businesses that coloured folk owned in Toronto: the first ice company there, a barbershop and a bathhouse, and even a horse-drawn cab company. There were no segregated schools in Toronto, not like the one in Bloomfield.

"Don't ever think the world doesn't know about us. In the streets of Toronto, I have seen with my own eyes actors playing a slave's life based on a book. All the audience gasping and white folks weeping at the lives we've led."

We dropped our mouths open and looked at one another.

"Everywhere, from Boston to Montreal to Britain, people are reading about us in a book called *Uncle Tom's Cabin,* written by a white woman. But I want all of us to read the words of someone who was once a slave himself — Josiah Henson, living in nearby Dresden."

"Is *Uncle Tom's Cabin* true, sir?"

"This woman's book is a novel. Somewhat romantic. Nevertheless, it tells some of our story to the world. To know the truth, we need to read this." He held up a thin book. "Here is Josiah Henson's own book. An autobiography. A memoir of his life written nearly ten years ago. Shall I read some aloud?"

Heads nodded. Our group sat up straight-backed, hands folded together, a getting-ready hush blowing from desk to desk.

"The title is: *The Life of Josiah Henson, Formerly a Slave, Now an Inhabitant of Canada West, as Narrated by Himself.*"

The schoolmaster read for some time and then stopped in the middle of a sentence. Silence after the reading as if we were sitting inside a church. Not one of us stirred. Not one of us even blinked.

Beulah's hand rose up. "Did he get free, sir?"

"Ah, did anyone hear the clue given about the ending?" asked Mister Dillon.

"The subtitle, sir," Abigail answered. "It says 'formerly a slave.' Meaning he was once a slave but is no more."

"Well done. Once a slave but no more, same as most of us in this room right now. So, Beulah, did Mr. Henson get free?"

Beulah was wiggling in her seat like she was getting ready to dance. Her whole bottom lifted up. "Oh yes, sir! He is free. And I can't wait to hear how he does it."

In the world that was Canada, potato hills were sprouting, squash vines were creeping, and we soon would hear how the former slave who was once like us got free.

Chapter 30
ANNUS MIRABILIS

June 1858

IT'D BEEN WELL OVER A MONTH since my letter was mailed. I thought my words would fly. But in truth, it seemed to take as long to go those miles and look for Pa as it did for us to journey from Georgia to Canada. What could happen to a letter? Maybe it never got there. Maybe it never had the right postage, although the postmaster glued it on himself. Maybe it got lost in the snow up in Collingwood, where they say winter lingered longer than here. Every time I saw the postmaster, I asked him if he had a letter for me, and when he said no I asked if it was sent proper. He swore it was. Now, as soon as he saw me coming, he turned the other way, those hands of his suddenly very busy.

Maybe Pa was no longer even there. If Levi and I walked up north next month, we might not find him.

At dusk, when nobody could see me, I stood by the edge of the fields where you had a clear view of the land in all directions. The sinking sun spilled pink into the sky then. And I faced east looking for Grandpa, then northeast searching for Pa. All I had inside me now was words. They leaped out of me: *I'm waitin' on you. Come!*

Mister Dillon taught me to believe in words. Words are their own candles. I prayed they'd find their way across the miles and months into listening ears.

* * *

184

Then one afternoon at school everything changed in a few seconds. The schoolmaster told us he was leaving Buxton. No longer would he teach at the Mission School.

"*Annus mirabilis!*" Mister Dillon announced. "A year of wonders. This is what it has been for me over this past year to teach those of you who once were slaves. I know now that we can do anything we set our minds to. You have taught me this."

Beulah cried. "But, sir, why must you leave? Where will you go?"

"Toronto," our schoolmaster said. "I've just taken a teaching position at a college. Perhaps I'll be teaching one of you there someday."

Tears ran down most girls' faces. Emanuel too would be leaving to attend Knox College in Toronto, to become a teacher like Mister Dillon. I'd learned enough of leave-takings to know that pieces of the schoolmaster would always stay with me. It was Mister Dillon who first drilled letters into my mind so my hand would know what to do. From not knowing one letter to reciting poems, it had been a year of wonders for me too since I crossed into Canada.

After I shook Mister Dillon's hand to say goodbye, he passed me Josiah Henson's book. He had just finished reading it aloud yesterday.

"This is a gift for you, Solomon. May you always remember how the world will open once you claim your own freedom, just as Josiah did."

I thanked him. We walked down the road together and I watched my schoolmaster leave. Josiah Henson's thoughts were held in my hands, the long trail of his words all saved inside the pages, telling how he found himself so free, he kissed Fort Erie ground as soon as he crossed over. I hugged the book straight to my chest so the words would fly right into me. And although I couldn't read most of it by myself yet, I trusted that it held within all the secrets of my own heart.

* * *

From the parlour each night, I could hear soft talk and quiet laughter, the way Levi and Isabella got when they were together. I sat alone in my room by candlelight and read my new book one word at a time. It was the first book I ever owned, maybe the only book in any nearby cabin other than the Bible. Some scenes I remembered clearly and that helped me understand the words. Some pages I skipped. Every paragraph or so I stopped because so many pictures swirled in my mind that I wanted to take a look at what was appearing. I saw the South clear. I saw the runaways hiding. I saw them crossing over as if I was there. Josiah sure had a way of telling words.

So many voices in my head.

Already, warnings were whispered among us about the new schoolmaster, Mister Crow, who had been spotted strutting down the road.

"Watch out. He's got a cane," Abigail said.

"What a terrible name he has!" David said. "I bet he'll be awful."

I didn't want to give a listen to them. I could be free, I decided, no matter if the schoolmaster was the Devil himself. For I'd been schooled by Mister Dillon.

Who would I listen to when I felt alone? The nightmares that yanked at me? Levi, who said Grandpa wouldn't be coming back? Or that voice that spoke to me out of nowhere as if it was alive? Never often enough, but always making me feel that I'd hear from Grandpa someday. So, if that's all I had — that voice — even if Grandpa never came back, at least I had that. Same as waiting for a letter from Pa. It was something to hope for.

Late on that warm night, I heard it for the first time — the whistle of the train along the Great Western Railway as it rattled through Chatham. You hardly ever heard it over in Buxton, I'd been told, except on windless summer nights. Its foggy voice reminded me of times in Little Africa when I heard it every single day, speeding across this free country. It called to me now from the distance, like an old friend.

Hold to those promises, it said.

Chapter 31
RING THOSE BELLS

Mid-July 1858

THE LOUD RINGING OF THE CHURCH BELL interrupted the morning lesson. We stopped and gave thanks for whoever had reached Buxton that day. Mister Crow changed the tally on the blackboard: *761*, it read. But after that, the day was long. The new schoolmaster seemed to think that keeping us in line and sitting straight-backed was his only job. His cane was swirling plenty.

By lunchtime, I'd rather have been bored than to hear what he said next.

There was a knock at the front schoolhouse door. A monitor went to answer and he came running back to whisper in the schoolmaster's ear.

"Solomon!" Mister Crow announced in a very loud voice. "Reverend King is at the door to see you."

Each pencil stopped. A murmur cloud spread across the room. Heads began to turn and look my way. I sat still as a fly on a crumb.

"Do you hear me, Solomon?" the schoolmaster's voice boomed.

I sprung up. Reverend King had never called on just *one* student at school before. He was the boss of the whole place. He came to see all the students working, and came here often enough that he knew everything was going right. Everything that was going *wrong* too. Had he guessed it was me who

188

carved *I luv Zemenia* on the inner wall of the outhouse? Nobody else knew. I thought it was my secret.

The schoolmaster flicked his cane, meaning for me to get moving. So I turned around and headed toward the door with heavy boots. My whole body trembled like I was going to Judgement Day at the end of the world. I'd never be the same once I went through that door. All those eyes from the other children heating up my back. Mister Crow's sour-lemon turned-down lips. What would such a powerful man as Reverend King give me as punishment? Maybe he'd put me in charge of scrubbing the outhouse floors so clean you could lick them.

"Solomon," Reverend King's voice boomed. "I thought this important enough not to wait."

"What have I done, sir?"

I looked up at Reverend King standing on the porch and saw the other man standing beside him. That man and I looked straight at one another. He stared and I stared back like I was tree sap sticking to each and every detail. The flat brown of his almond eyes. The ears sticking out too large for his head. The heart shape of his face with its pointy chin. It felt like I was looking in a mirror.

"That's my boy, Solomon. At last," my pa said. "How he's grown."

He drew me into him and I held still and breathed. I shut my eyes and travelled so far back in an instant. Way back to the days when Pa still walked beside me. Him showing me where the rabbits hid or how to tell what kind of hawk was sailing high and even how to catch a fish with your bare hands. Nights when I'd cry because my fingers were so scraped raw by the cotton boles and his hands tickled light through my hair, slowing my breath and my tears, setting me to sleep. The touch of his rough hands, so light, as if I was something precious and fragile like broken glass, and he was mending me back together again.

With that, I popped open my eyes. It was real. Pa's hands were on my head. I saw the trees right above my head and the road and wondered where I was at. This was Buxton, though it did not seem the same. This was the same earth I'd been living on all these months. I stared again at my pa and felt no time at all had passed between us. Here he was right in front of me. All my life I'd been looking for words, just the right ones, and now I had no need of any at all.

"This boy makes me proud," said Reverend King. "When he arrived this winter, he could neither read or write. Never imagined himself that he could do either one. But his written words have brought his father from out of the wilderness to find him. Remarkable!"

Then I remembered the Liberty Bell. That morning when it sounded, it had rung for my own pa! It was still singing inside me, tolling in such a deep-down place where all my words and all my hope had been stalled, waiting for him. Everything burst out of me like an explosion. I danced and hopped all around Pa like some leapfrog. My feet wouldn't keep still any longer.

"Pa!" I yelled out loud. "You're here!"

He dug into his pocket and showed me the letter, folded many times, that I had sent him. "You called me here with this, son. Though I cannot read or write, folks in my community could. They came lookin' for me. Soon as I read it, I packed my belongings and left there for good to come find you."

"Tell the boy where you've been all this time, Isam," Reverend King said.

"When I first crossed over from Detroit into Canada, I roamed all around, even to Buxton. I wanted to forget slavery, to forget how it wasn't safe to take my own boy out. I wanted to be in a quiet place. So I went north. Couldn't get land in the Queen's Bush anymore, so I kept walking and eventually ended up in Collingwood and found work near there. But I never forgot you, Solomon. Or how I left you behind."

"But you thought you were leavin' me safe with Grandpa."

"Let's go get your grandpa now. We'll surprise him good. Where's he at?"

My stomach churned. It took a while to get my breath. When I told Pa what had happened, I hoped he wouldn't blame me.

"Wish I had gone back to bring you both across," was all he said, his voice low. "Your grandpa would be with us still. And you'd have been free for some years too."

He asked all about Grandpa then and I told him all I knew and how I'd been waiting for his return. Reverend King looked so quiet as he listened.

"We'll pray for him until we have word of him," he said. "Those bells will be ringing for him each morning and evening of every day."

Then Pa looked at me. "I hung my head down this whole time for leavin' you behind, son. Begged forgiveness at every church I passed through. Your letter came like grace to save me. I told myself it's a sign God forgave me. But . . . do you?"

I never really dared dream of seeing my pa again. Nobody came back from freedom, the old ones back home said. Yet here, in this new land, are mysteries like how my written words found Pa while he was busy searching for me in his own heart.

I grinned wide as I could. My mouth never felt so big. It was big as Levi's. "We are together now, Pa. I'm gonna forget real quick all we went through."

Reverend King led us both into the schoolroom to stand up in front. He made a speech to all the students about how my pa had just arrived and been reunited with me. "Such is the power of words. Of reading and writing," he announced. "If one letter can bring about such a miracle, think what all your schooling will do."

The whole class clapped their hands. All those shiny faces were looking at us and rejoicing with me like they really were my brothers and sisters. Beulah and Zemenia both had tears running down their cheeks. Even Mister Crow sucked in his lips and smiled. I was standing up in front of everybody and loved it; I even smiled. Best of all, Reverend King excused me from school for the rest of the day to be with Pa.

Pa! You're here!

I grabbed Pa's arm and skipped down the schoolhouse steps. We found Old Ezekiel right away, walking slow through the cemetery stones nearby.

"Look!" I called to him. "It's my pa, Isam. You helped me find him."

He and my pa shook hands. We both thanked Old Ezekiel, who nodded his head. He rewarded us with a soft look over his lined face.

Buxton was filled with smiles that day. Everyone who passed by, we told our story to. I couldn't take my eyes off Pa. Some moments it seemed impossible that he was right there beside me. But the next minute it seemed he had never been gone at all.

Then we walked the concession road to find Levi. Some afternoons that spring, he and Will left work early and took turns axing down trees on one another's land. Today they were both hoeing the vegetables on Levi's land. Cabbage and turnip leaves popped up between the tree stumps. Isabella was there too with a picnic lunch she had just spread out. Purple phlox leaped from the garden in front of our cabin.

Pa immediately pumped Levi's hand up and down real fast. But suddenly his hand froze and he just stared at Levi. "You *that* boy?" he gasped. "The one in the woods at night behind Tiller's?"

Levi dropped Pa's hand. "How did you . . . were *you* there?"

"I hid in that dugout for weeks with another man. Told to wait there by a conductor. Master's men were searching everywhere for me. It wasn't safe to leave. I wouldn't have made it out without your help. You fed us both."

"You two knew each another?" I blurted out. "When? What happened?"

I looked back and forth between the two of them. They didn't seem to see me or hear any of my questions. Both seemed like strangers to me.

Isabella walked over to Levi. "Go ahead. Tell. It's all right now."

"I never really saw you or the others out there. It was so dark," Levi said. "And I begged you not to tell me your names in case I was caught. Got real good at takin' food from the plantation. Watered milk down. Slipped eggs out of the barn. Even took a pig."

"You mean there were others hidin' out there after we left?"

Levi nodded. "Runaways used that hidin' spot. Even though takin' food was a crime in the master's eyes, I helped them out for years. I even dreamed I'd go north some day too. Because I did that and then ran off, slavecatchers followed us. We would have crossed safe by ferry, like we planned, if I hadn't done that. Jacob would be with us now. Every time I looked at Solomon on our journey, I felt sorry for what I did."

My pa shook his head. "You risked your life for those runaways. For me. To those livin' out there, it kept us strong so we could run. And you brought my son to freedom. If anyone did wrong, it was me. I abandoned my own boy."

Isabella stepped right between Pa and Levi, grabbing both of their arms. "Don't talk like this! You both did what had to be done at the time. No right or wrong in that. Reverend King said we may have done terrible things to get free. But it's what we *had* to do. Such hurt comes from slavery. He said we got to forget and forgive everyone, even our masters. But most of all, ourselves."

Pa turned to me. "My son says he forgives me. The rest is up to God. And we owe you so much, Levi, for takin' care of my boy and bringin' him across."

"Solomon?" Levi grinned. "If he hadn't bossed me so much, we would have got to Buxton a whole lot sooner."

We all laughed at that. Soon we were sitting in the shade of the lone oak by Levi's cabin, sipping lemon balm tea and gulping down roast chicken. Every once in a while, Levi looked over at Pa and just shook his head, remembering. Will brought some new radish and red oak lettuce. Isabella handed us a treat when our lunch was done. Gingerbread! I ate it twice at Christmas before. You don't forget that taste. Spicy and sweet. Soft and spongy. You chew and chew and still got some ginger sizzling like fire in your mouth.

I took it from her hand, closed my eyes and chewed. And the memory of the South burst wide open, how this gingerbread was the one sweet thing I ever had in slavery. On Christmas, the whole day long was free of work, and filled with laughter. A roasted pig cooking all day on a spit. Gingerbread heating our mouths. And the evening spent watching holiday lights in the big house shine across the way like a bright promise.

"I never had more than one slice of this cake a year. Bet if I eat another one right now — " I teased Isabella, to see what she would do " — it'll make me wild!"

She smiled and handed me another piece of gingerbread. As soon as I was done chewing, I lit up, flew to my feet and turned somersaults all over the ground.

Pa started laughing, slapping his thighs just like Grandpa did after a good joke. Will was grinning. Levi laid right down between the cabbage plants and hooted to the sky while Isabella giggled, tears rolling down her face, and held her belly hard.

"Can they hear us all the way down South?" I shouted.

Freedom was so simple. Freedom was eating gingerbread on an ordinary weekday right in the middle of the field. Freedom was laughing until your belly hurt. Freedom was being with friends and family.

Pa! You're here!

Chapter 32
IF THOUGHTS HAD WINGS

Late July 1858

ALL THIS TIME, I'd been searching north for Pa and east for Grandpa. Looking both ways, I was stuck in the middle, alone. Now that Pa had come, I slipped into him easy as a second skin. I was home. Come evening, it was him and me walking in line with other adults down to Reverend King's house. We'd all hover in the sitting room with books on our laps while Reverend King read aloud to us. My fingers paused at the words on the page while Pa listened. He studied my face while we worked, amazed at how the strange words fell from my lips reciting in time with Reverend King. I even taught Pa to spell his own name. When he saw me write it out the first time, he shook his head in amazement.

"You learned so much, so quick too. Nobody gave you much of a chance, son. You did it on your own."

When lessons were done, it was already dark. Pa held a pine knot high to light our way the three miles back along Centre Road.

"We got a new life together in this country, son," Pa said. "Ain't no more lookin' back now that you and me are together again. Havin' a family, some land of my own, and a son learnin', is all a man could want."

I turned to him then and told him about one more looking-back thing — the last time I saw Grandpa, and all the nightmares I'd had of his hand in the air, waving one last time, over a year ago.

"Your Grandpa wasn't sayin' goodbye. He must have been in

196

such pain, didn't want you to see. All he could think about was gettin' healed. Wish I'd been there with you. I'd have told you to go on, just like he did."

Let's find him ... I didn't dare say those words aloud to Pa yet. Some things you don't talk about. I'd learned that with Levi. Did no good to whine. But I decided to ask something now.

"What can we do about Grandpa?"

"That I've been thinkin' on, Sol. Give me time and we'll see what can be done. Maybe a letter like you sent me. Or perhaps someone from Buxton may be travellin' that way. Meantime, let's think about settlin' here and buyin' land, though I have little money."

Sometimes, at dusk, Pa and Old Ezekiel took long walks through the fields, passing between the tall cornstalks. I could see just their heads moving along. At that time of day, the stalks whispered as they leaned against one another, telling us work was at an end. I knew Pa and the elder were talking about a way to find someone who is lost. It must be Grandpa they were speaking about. Once or twice Pa looked up to find me staring at him across the fields. We fixed our attention straight on one another the way Grandpa Jacob and I used to do from far away. No talking in the fields was the rule back then. So my thoughts flew out of me right to Pa like they had wings.

Now that you're here, we can find a way to Grandpa. If we don't hear about him soon, we may lose him forever.

Pa kept on walking ahead with Old Ezekiel. I wondered if he heard me at all.

* * *

One Saturday morning, two weeks after Pa arrived, he and I were hoeing Will's vegetable patch while Will went off to help Levi clear more fields. I loved being out there with the corn growing nearby. It seemed so alive, almost like it could talk. Early that morning, it dropped dew like petals of sweat. By noon, the stalks were so full of sun, I swear they grew an inch a minute. They leaped up tall, rattling their heads, sizzling like bacon in a pan.

By then it was so stifling hot in the field, it reminded us of Georgia. We both took off our shirts and wrapped bandannas around our heads to keep off the sun. Pa bent over the collards and hoed. Over his bare back were markings, rippled and dark. Old whippings, too many to count. They snaked from his shoulders to his waist.

All at once, I started shaking from the top of my head down through my legs. I saw it all clear, that night he came back . . .

Blood dripped onto the floor. Thick and red, it poured out. Pa reeled from side to side, propped up by two strong field hands. I didn't recognize Pa's face. It was all twisted, with his eyes shut tight. Then his knees buckled and he went down to the floor, the men breaking his fall, easing him slowly. That's when I saw his back. The skin shredded and hanging like butchered meat. The raw red of the inside of him, bone poking through, and all that blood . . .

"It *was* you, wasn't it?" I breathed. "No dream at all. It was *you* who got hurt."

Pa nodded his head and stopped hoeing. "Doesn't hurt anymore. It healed up long ago. I was hopin' you wouldn't remember. You were so young. Your Grandpa carried you away and you slept in another cabin for weeks while I healed."

"When did you run?"

"Soon as I could stand. About a month afterwards. I asked them to bring you by . . . I wanted you to have one last night to remember me by."

"You got whipped almost to death. Why did they do that?"

"For sneakin' water to Eli. He was chained to the barn three hot days without food or water for not pickin' enough cotton." He slammed his fist on his leg. "Anytime they wanted, they could hurt us. Maybe even kill us. When somebody has that kind of power over you, you are nobody. I *had* to run — "

Someone was shouting from the road.

"Isam! Come quick! Run to Levi's! There's big trouble over there."

We flew across the road. Up ahead stood a crowd of settlers around Levi's cabin. Two white strangers stepped out of a wagon. Levi stood alone facing them. His hands were clenched and he was breathing hard.

"There he is! That's Levi of Tiller plantation. He's a thief and a murderer!" The two men pointed. "We come for him."

A murmur rippled through the crowd.

"No! It's not true!" someone shouted.

"Tell us what he did then," ordered another.

"Why, he stole food belonging to Master Tiller. That's a crime in Georgia. And he killed a man while he was escaping. Look at the size of that Levi. He could knock somebody dead in a second. He's dangerous. You folks are fortunate that we come to take him away."

"Let's hear from Levi," Will demanded.

Pa and I rushed over and stood on either side of Levi to face the strangers.

"I took food, yes," he said. "That's all. Plenty of extra food at Tiller's. Master was rich. And his slaves were starvin'."

"Who did you feed, Levi?" Isabella broke through the crowd and yelled.

"Me!" Pa shouted. "I was a runaway hidin' in the woods with

wounds that had not healed. If Levi hadn't fed me, I'd have died out there."

From behind us, we heard wagon wheels screeching to a halt.

"You think a slave's life is worth something?" Reverend King called to the strangers.

"Sure do. Levi's worth seven hundred dollars to capture alive and return to Georgia. That's because he murdered the day he left. Strangled the overseer and left him in the dirt."

The crowd gasped and turned to look at one another, then back at Levi. These strangers were slavecatchers and somehow they had tracked Levi here where we all thought we were safe. And they came with accusations about one of us, the worst crime there was: murder.

It wasn't true!

Words buzzed out of me like yellowjackets swarming straight at the strangers.

"It's a lie! I was with Levi the day he left. He took me and Grandpa Jacob with him. All he did was take three apples, no more. We waited 'til dark and sneaked past the overseer standin' on patrol in the yard with his gun. He never saw us leave."

Reverend King shouted. "Is this true, Levi?"

Levi gasped. "I never hurt anyone in my whole life. All I did wrong was take some food."

"You heard Levi. We have laws in Canada," Reverend King told the slavecatchers. "Even if your master took his claim on Levi to the highest court here, that court would clear him. If something was stolen to aid escape, that was no crime. For a man owns his own self, body and soul. Besides, once Levi stepped over the border, he was legally free. You have no right to him."

All the folk from Buxton sighed with relief.

"This man is no murderer, as you falsely accuse. But you and your kind are," Reverend King continued. "You enslave others. That is most certainly a crime in *this* country."

Silence. All eyes shifted to the strangers. The two white men began to step backwards, toward their wagon. One looked for an opening in the crowd, but there was none.

Reverend King shouted so all could hear. "Who would like to help me lead these slavecatchers straight to Chatham and make certain they board the next train to Detroit?"

The circle of men and women around the strangers tightened. Will held onto the horse's bridle so he could steer it slow. Scowling, the two men boarded their wagon. The crowd headed with them to the train station in Chatham.

Isabella ran over to Levi. "Now do you see? You committed no crime. And no one will hunt you down anymore. You are free forevermore. And you are the bravest man I have ever met."

All the air went back into Levi and he stood tall. The biggest grin lit his face. "Does this mean you will marry me?"

Isabella gasped.

Levi lifted her up in his arms and swung her high. The rest of us standing there cheered as we heard Isabella's "Yes!"

Beulah danced round them in circles.

Pa elbowed me and winked. "Told you they were courtin', didn't I?"

Afterwards, Levi shook Pa's hand and then mine. "You came to my rescue, Isam. I am most thankful. You and your son are living proof of what I did. Even Reverend King himself said I did no wrong. So now I got to tell you my plans for us all."

Pa and I looked sideways at one another. Levi was up to one

of his schemes again. I wondered if I should start running now. Instead, it was Levi who rushed off into the cabin and returned, breathless, his hands in his pockets.

"I spoke to the association here in Buxton. They said it's all right my givin' you that plot of ten acres right over there, since we are almost family." Levi pointed to the woods right next to his cabin. "You and Sol will be our neighbours. And here's the nine dollars Sol earned, enough for you to buy some tools."

Levi handed the money to me in silver dollars. I slipped it right into Pa's hands.

"Why, Levi, I . . . I don't know what to say. It's like you've been readin' my mind. Sol and I were just talkin' about settlin' down here. But I can't take it for free."

"You gonna take it. So much has been given me after such a hard life that all I wanna do is make sure everyone feels the same way as I do."

"Sol has been like a son to me," Isabella said. "Already you are family. So, please come and live next to us."

Pa finally said yes and we all cheered. He'd sign the deed soon with his own written name — after I read it, of course. We stood and looked over at the ten acres and made plans for clearing it soon as we could.

The next day was Sunday and we all headed to church to hear Reverend King tell about how the strong arms of those who were once slaves held all of us safe yesterday and made certain that Levi was free. He thanked all the men and women who had stood by and not let the slavecatchers succeed. I gave thanks too. I wouldn't have to worry about Pa getting hurt anymore. He'd healed up. There'd be no more nightmares to haunt me now.

Pa and I walked away silently when the service was done. All around us were laughter and celebration and even hats flying in the air. But neither of us felt free and light, the way Reverend King said we ought to feel. He even said we have wings now. But Pa and I didn't. Because one of us was left behind and we didn't know if he was living or dead, on the way to us, or sent back to slavery.

Let's go find him. We gotta go now . . .

Words were filling me up to the brim and Pa had to know now. "We made a zigzag trail across Canada, Pa. How can Grandpa ever find us in Buxton?"

"It's us who's gonna find him, son."

I stared at Pa. Had he heard the voice speaking inside me? Or the words floating his way across the wide fields every single day?

"Not safe to send a letter to Bertie Hall or the Buffalo church," Pa went on. "Old Ezekiel said it might alert folks that such places hide slaves. So we'll go to Fort Erie ourselves. We are sure to hear news of your grandpa there. Once we find him and bring him home, he'll tell us when to plant fall collards and mustard greens. Besides, it's your birthday time. You were born thirteen years ago at the end of July. This is your present. I hear there's a way to travel fast to Fort Erie."

"It took us a month or more to cross on foot, Pa. The only way to — " My whole body lit up. Pa was smiling at me. "You mean by *train!?*"

He nodded. "Got it all planned. We leave Tuesday."

I jumped up, grabbed someone's hat and flung it high. Suddenly I had turned thirteen years old and free at the same time. Pa and I joined the rest of Buxton celebrating our newfound freedom all over again.

Chapter 33
THE MORNING EXPRESS

JUMPING. MY FEET WERE LEAPING SO HIGH, my heels hit my behind. Butterflies were flying every which way inside my stomach and fluttering up to my throat. In the grey before Chatham's dawn, we were waiting on the 5:35 Morning Express Number 2 train. Levi and Will both gave us money for second-class tickets to board the Great Western Railway. And Isabella lent us Sunday clothes so we would look respectable and there'd be no trouble.

Pa and I were taking the train together. Listening for the faint far-off whistle like all those times I heard it in Little Africa. Only now a train was coming for *us*. Eight hours from Chatham to the City of the Falls, the stationmaster boasted. That's right where the great Falls were, on the Niagara River that I'd once crossed over. There, on the schedule posted on the wall, I was able to trace the numbers with my fingers and read them too. I could not believe it. It had taken us a month to cross the country by foot and slow wagon. That *afternoon*, we'd be seeing the Falls for the first time. By the next morning, we'd be at Bertie Hall.

The rails were singing. High notes ringing. The whistle screamed. It was coming.

Everyone flocked out of the station house. All heads turned. A long train snaked our way. Larger and larger it grew until at last it shuddered to a halt in front of us. Porters called "Get on

204

board!" Folks stepped up into the cars. Beneath my feet, the train heaved. It quivered. It shivered. It was puffing alive and I was on board at last. How it snorted when it started up again, blowing a huff of steam Chatham's way before it headed off. We barely had time to find a seat. My whole body bounced up and down the aisle before we plopped down together. That train shot along the rails so fast, my bones hummed.

We sat straight up with our mouths open and stared out the window. We faced north, the direction we were going. That way we could see the towns before we came upon them. All the forests and flat farmlands in between. Houses dotting the land. The whole of Canada West was laid out before us like a map.

Towns began to pass by. With great shuddering and shrieking of wheels, the train stopped at some, jerking us back and forth, then whizzed by others. Leaning around the bends, we were a part of its long body. Past Thamesville, Newbury, Longwood and then London for a longer stop. Ingersoll, Woodstock, Princeton, Paris, Copetown and Dundas. At Hamilton the train stopped for quite a while. Lots of folks got off and plenty more boarded. Mostly white, but not all — seems we lived everywhere across this country. Outside stretched a wide blue lake with grey haze upon it and gulls circling everywhere.

"That must be one of the great lakes Mister Dillon told us about, Pa! Lake Ontario. I can't believe this country has so much water."

"Good fishin' too!" said a man who just boarded.

My stomach began growling by then. Word about what the railroad conductor said had passed around the cabin: "No serving coloured folks in the dining car." Pa and I paid no mind. We had no extra money anyway. Nothing was going to stop us from enjoying the trip. Out of our pockets we took Isabella's lunch of turkey legs, small boiled red potatoes and cornbread.

Out the window, the lake barely left our side. It ran along with us, blue grey, gulls circling above it, all the way. Just like Lake Erie, it seemed to have no end or beginning. Between the lunch and staying awake most of the night waiting to leave, I got right sleepy. Being in the train was like sitting in a rocking chair that rocked all by itself. The blue of the lake whirring by at times hypnotized me.

I leaned against Pa and sighed. When you're with somebody from first light until it's time to sleep, memorizing their face, reading it to tell you everything you need to know, it gets easy between you. You become pals. I had never gotten to know my pa this way before. Little pieces of me sank into him for holding. Things I needed to know and never had anyone to ask. Like how my ma looked and what was the last thing she said before she was sold away. Winny, her name was. She was very small and thin. She yelled to Pa from the wagon carting her away, "Look for me in heaven when slavery will be done and gone. 'Til then, keep my boy safe."

Bit by bit, mile by mile, I told him my secrets and he told me his.

So many freedoms to want, one after another, like the many layers of an onion. Freedom to think your own thoughts. Freedom from hurt. Freedom to learn. Freedom to be with your family. When you get down to the core, you save it for what is most precious. For me, that's finally saying what's been locked tight in my heart. Letting it fly free from the deepdown places of me. Pa was holding it for me now, in safekeeping.

Stoney Creek. Grimsby. Beamsville. Jordan. The train turned south after St. Catharines. Within the hour, it slowed. Finally we were there, at the Clifton Railway station. It was the end of the line for us. We ran off fast as we could to watch the train head toward the bridge. The suspension bridge floated right across the wide gap between Canada West and New York. It didn't sway but held on tight. Right in front of our eyes, the Number 2 train slipped onto other rails and crawled across the top of the bridge. My heart leaped. A mile of empty space lay beneath it. Cliff and rock poked out everywhere. Far beneath was the wild water I'd once crossed, the Niagara River.

"Look! Below the train!" Pa called out.

We stood with a flock of folks, all tourists in Sunday clothes, looking up. For the bridge had two parts, one for the trains high above and another for carriages below. Folks were even walking across it. This was the same bridge Mr. Sims from Buxton said he had walked across into Canada one night. When he was halfway across, he actually stopped and screamed for joy, way up high. If we had escaped this way, I'd never have walked across here. Just to look down now, from the safety of the cliff above, made me gasp. Then we turned south towards the Falls. The winds were whirling and roaring and we saw them at once: all the falls, for there seemed more than one. Three falls shot down hard without pause over sharp cliffs. They made an ear-splitting sound. By the time we got to them, we could only hear each other if we shouted, though we stood side by side. We leaned against rock and railings with our faces and clothes all damp from the spitting of water. We must have stood there for hours, watching.

"Horseshoe Falls!" yelled a tour guide, who told us he'd worked in Little Africa before. "It belongs to Canada and it's the biggest. The Bridal Veil Falls over there is small. The other one is in New York."

This was the noise we'd heard that night in the back of the wagon, water rushing louder and louder until it thundered in our ears. The drivers must have thought of holding us at the border town that night, where others might have helped them tie us down. Such a remembering took hold of me. There were no words for what happened that night, how all our plans exploded, how Grandpa and I were split apart, and how I lived ever after, leaning to the other side. I thought I had told Pa everything. But there was more inside me, waiting.

In front of us appeared so many wonders. Tourist hotels. Fancy white folks served by waiters whose dark faces shone above their starchy white shirts. Horse-drawn carriages filled with tourists. Their upright drivers nodded greetings to us like we were old friends. How fine and strong these men looked, nothing like Levi and I, beaten-down and starving, when we first crossed over. The world had changed in thirteen months. Those who might have once been slaves were safe, free and working near the border crossing.

We ate the last of our food and headed south along the road. The river ran right beside us all the while, wild and rushing down to the Falls behind our backs. I kept turning my head to watch the Niagara River until my stomach began to churn too. As the miles passed, changing from late afternoon to evening, we grew tired. The closer we came to Bertie Hall, the more unease I felt. Was I giving up on finding Grandpa, I wondered. Would we get there and hear bad news?

Then I saw it. "There, Pa! Up ahead!"

I pointed out Bertie Hall. No mistaking its white pillars shining even in the dark. I turned to look at the swirling Niagara River that once I'd crossed right here. My heart pumped quicker and quicker. There, in the mists, I thought I saw an arm raised up clawing air. A head bobbing up and down. Then it disappeared.

I could have drowned here. Or been caught by slavecatchers and dragged back home. I could have died here.

Then I remembered all those ghosts that had appeared. I too had been a shadow, a slave boy on the plantation who learned that following orders kept him alive. As long as I was invisible, I was safe. I had still lived like that for many months in Canada. Half free on this side, I still had not crossed over to being myself true and free.

I plunked right down on the ground. All this time waiting on Grandpa, half of me tried to step ahead without him while the other half stayed behind. Couldn't go forward and couldn't go back.

Then I heard his voice and it seemed like a dream.

"Son? Solomon! What's wrong? Tell me."

My lips started moving although I was cold through and through. "On the other side . . . was . . . It's where we left Grandpa and where I . . . " I could barely say the words. " . . . where I left myself. I have been living here all this time half alive."

A sound came out of Pa, almost like a cry. He sat right down and set my head to his chest. I could hear his heart throbbing hard, galloping right into my ears.

"You are safe now, son. At last. How I've grieved that I could not have been with you then. You were on your own much too long. But I'm here to stay now."

He rocked back and forth. We both grew quiet and all was calm.

"Sol, I felt the same," he whispered to me. "Like I was disappearin'. Skin over a bag of bones. My own body carried me around, but inside I was dead. I lost who Isam was. You said it true. That's how slavery made us feel. But slavery is done now. So we got to keep our eyes to the road ahead."

I sat up and looked at him. Pa had lived in freedom longer than me. He seemed more like a tree now. Still and waiting. Looking straight ahead.

"It's all ahead of us now," he said. "A new life in Buxton and maybe findin' your grandpa too."

The Niagara River was swirling below us. Tossing and spitting and full of mists rising. I watched that fog lift and spread like ghost feet. The ghost of me once floated in that river, drifted to the other side and clung to Grandpa. But I wasn't that same boy anymore. I'd been living in a free village in a free country. I'd learned to read and write some. More than the world had changed in these thirteen months. I was different too. Pa was beside me now and I myself wrote the words that set him free to fly to me.

It was too late to approach Bertie Hall. Nearby was a field of high corn. Into it we slipped, laying our tarp flat on the dewy ground. We sank down. All night long, the river called.

There will be one more ghost, it said. *And then no more.*

Chapter 34
"KEEP WALKIN'"

End of July 1858

WE SNEAKED INTO THE YARD AT DAWN and dared knock by the servants' entrance at the side of Bertie Hall. A woman answered, told us to wait, and went to find her mistress.

Missus Forsyth finally stood in the doorway.

"I'm Isam, ma'am," Pa said. "I never met you, but you gave my boy shelter."

She peered at me. "Are you that same boy who crossed over last June?"

"I am Solomon, ma'am. Not the same but still me."

She clasped her hands to her heart. "I never imagined such a bright face before on a runaway. How you have changed! You've grown half a foot and are filling out that suit of clothes most fine. How pleased I am to see you so well and healthy."

"We came to thank you, ma'am," Pa continued. "And also to find Jacob, my boy's grandfather. He was supposed to come over here soon as he healed, late last fall."

Missus Forsyth frowned. "Are you certain he knew to come to Bertie Hall? We have had no word of him. Many fugitives passed through here these last months. But no older man."

Pa and I stood with our caps in our hands and silence in our empty hearts.

Missus Forsyth gave an order to her maid and then turned to us. "Spend the night here. We'll fix you a meal. We can sit down and talk over what to do next."

211

Pa raised his head. "I've already decided, ma'am. Gonna cross over to the church in Buffalo. Board that ferry even if I am the only runaway to travel back. Find out where my pa Jacob went. He must be healed and on his way. That church will know."

This was the first I'd heard of such a plan. It was all wrong. Dangerous too. Pa seemed so determined to track Grandpa, he wasn't thinking clear.

"It's best to think things over on a full belly," Missus Forsyth insisted. "You both need rest after your trip. Come morning, you'll decide what to do."

So Pa and I spent the day at Bertie Hall. We ate and later dozed in the yard, where the servants left us black tea with berries and scones. We even chuckled some about being tourists. It was a slow, silent summer's day. I sat listening to the roar of the river and the carriages rolling past on the street. Finally, at night, we stepped into the cellar to sleep.

It was cool and dark down there. The two cots waited. So strange to see Pa stretch out on the cot Levi once took. If only Pa had been with me that night, we never would have left Grandpa Jacob behind.

If only . . .

I drifted and fell into a deep sleep. My body seemed to lift up and leave the rest of me behind on the cot. The bolted door to the tunnel loomed ahead. Through that door my body floated like fog. In my dream, I searched for one face . . .

"Where is Grandpa?" I called out.

Echoes flew back at me like a hundred bats screeching: *Grandpa! Grandpa! Grandpa!* The walls were slimy and closing in. It got very cold. I could hear Rodney's breathing, hard and raspy. He was pacing the tunnel back and forth, back and forth, wringing his hands and moaning. You don't ever want to see a ghost fussing like that.

He turned my way. "Where have you been?"

"In Buxton. Readin' and writin'."

"You mean books? You've been reading them? I never read anymore. If I could, maybe I'd forget this torment of living in a tunnel, wanting to get out to freedom. If only I could read again."

"I could read to you right now if you like."

My hand pressed my chest to see if it was still there, flat inside my shirt where I'd kept it since it was given to me. I pulled it out, my book about Josiah Henson. "Here is the story of a slave who crossed over to Fort Erie, Rodney. Listen."

Between the words I read aloud, I looked up now and again. After several pages, Rodney sat down. By the middle of the book, he had closed his eyes. He was breathing slow and deep by the time I'd read most of the book and I thought he was asleep. So I stopped reading. His eyes immediately flew open. Dark and rimmed with white. He bowed his head to thank me.

"People do get freedom, even if they have to wait a long time. Both this man and you, Solomon, are free. Perhaps I could be free one day too."

"You can be free any time you decide. For you are long dead and can leave, Rodney. Your pa and ma are no longer livin'. They are waitin' for you to cross over."

"Where are they?"

I swallowed hard. "On the other side. They passed and are waitin'."

Rodney yawned. "I'll go find them then; I can go to sleep now. But you must promise me something. Not you or your father should step foot on that far shore again. If you ever want to grow up with your own father, don't let him cross."

How did this ghost know about Pa's plans? I thought ghosts lived only in the past. Maybe they could see the future too. If there was danger ahead, Rodney surely would know of it.

"But Pa wants to cross over where it isn't safe. He says he is not free unless his own pa is free. I can't lose Pa! Not when I just found him."

"Look elsewhere, in the world you knew, and you shall find the old one you seek."

When I woke up, my body felt light and loose, as if everything in the world was lifting up and getting free. *There will be one more ghost,* I'd been told that night we slept beside the river. *And then no more.* All the ghosts were gone now. I had evened the debt I owed Rodney. He was finally sleeping when the dream ended. Whatever ghosts had haunted me in Canada and in the South were floating away.

But as soon as Missus Forsyth called us up the stairs, Pa insisted on his plans to cross over the Niagara River by ferry. He tipped his cap and began walking toward the door. How could I tell him about my dream and about meeting up with Rodney last night and all those warnings he gave me? Such things were fearsome to speak about and Pa might not believe me at all. We'd been together for such little time. If he went away now, I might never see him again.

Don't let him cross! a voice warned inside me.

I stood in the doorway and blocked the way out. Pa kept walking ahead. I took hold of his shirt and tugged, then dropped down to the floor, wrapped my arms around his legs and held on with all my might.

"Don't go back! It's not safe! Remember what I told you happened to Adam!" I burst out. "Besides, we haven't even searched Little Africa yet. Maybe Grandpa Jacob found some other place to cross over, and he's right there, lookin' for us."

"The boy's right," Missus Forsyth said. "There's so many ways he could have crossed this river — at the suspension bridge or one of the many ferries. I don't like hearing about your travelling out in the open aboard a ferry. Try this side of the river first. Besides, it's Emancipation Day all over Canada today, don't you know? Go celebrate first."

"All right. We'll go over to Little Africa," Pa finally said. "But, if there's no word of him, then I cross over by myself."

Though Missus Forsyth offered to send us in her carriage, I refused. I wanted to stretch the time out that I still had with Pa, slow him down and look for signs of Grandpa along the way. Surely someone had noticed him in these parts. As soon as he came over, he would have mentioned my name and Levi's too and someone might have told him we'd been here. I stepped down hard, booted feet hugging free brown soil.

The moment we headed away from the river and down the street, I heard it.

Come, the voice called.

My head lifted right up. I had not heard that voice in a long, long while.

Keep walkin', the voice rose up inside me.

It was an old voice, steady and strong as my own heartbeat.

I set my boots down flat and walked on ahead with Pa.

Chapter 35
EMANCIPATION DAY

August 1, 1858

I BEGAN TO LOOK at every passerby closely. Any stranger I saw, I stopped and asked if they'd seen Grandpa. But, one by one, each stranger shook their head and walked on.

Suddenly I was aware that Pa was not looking straight ahead like me, toward Little Africa. He had turned around to study the river. He stood still in the middle of the road and didn't say anything, I knew what he was thinking — that it's easy to cross here, it's not that wide.

Didn't he remember the stories passed down by the old ones back home who said we had once crossed over waters to get to this country? They whispered that we left our souls back there in our homeland. *Once you cross over, you are never the same*, they warned.

We'd crossed over once. That was enough. We weren't allowed to go back to the United States. Ever.

I called his name to come follow me.

Pa murmured, "It's so close. Seems a shame to go to some village to celebrate with folks we don't know when we do know where Grandpa was stayin'. If it's not safe to travel by ferry, bet I could swim across tonight."

I tugged on his arm. "No, Pa! You don't know that river. It's tricky, full of wild water pullin' you downstream. Besides, you agreed to look here first. That's what you told Missus Forsyth."

But Pa did not move ahead. "I could go — "

216

On all sides, crowds of people from Little Africa, plus a few white people, were walking, filling the road and paths. Some seemed in a hurry. Most were smiling. Children were skipping. The adults nodded at us.

"You headed to Little Africa?" I shouted to one woman.

She called back. "Sure am. Been waitin' on this day. Parade's gonna start soon."

"Have you seen any old man crossed over lately? Been searchin' for my Grandpa Jacob."

"Jacob? Don't know anybody by that name." She shook her head.

By then, wagonloads of townspeople rolled past us, all headed to Little Africa.

Pa watched everyone on the road. "Never would have guessed so many of us crossed over like this. Must be hundreds here who once lived as slaves, just like us."

I looked at all the bright faces of those who were free.

"JACOB!" I yelled. "From the TILLER plantation. All the way from Georgia. My grandpa! Has anyone seen him?"

I rushed ahead, shouting to all the wagons and the people in them. Someone had to know him. Most shook their heads. Some did not look down at me at all but only to the distant road, their eyes glowing. The crowd disappeared into the village of Little Africa. In her high carriage, Missus Forsyth passed us by, pointing to the road ahead with her gloved hand, her voice trailing after us.

"Come quickly! Don't miss the parade!"

I tugged Pa's sleeve. "She's waitin' on us. Let's show her we sure can celebrate the freedom this country gave us. If it weren't for her, I wouldn't be here now. Come!"

Pa faced ahead now. I had hold of his sleeve; I never wanted to let go of it. If he turned away right now, I'd drag him back.

Pa started walking on again. After a mile or so, around the next bend of the road, I saw where we were, Little Africa's cemetery. And then the voice reminded me: *Look elsewhere, in the world you knew, and you shall find the old one you seek.*

My boots stopped dead. *No! Not here! Please! Not here.*

I thought of Old Ezekiel wandering Buxton's cemetery in search of the names of those who died. I did not want to enter this cemetery, but Pa immediately headed into it. More wooden crosses stood now. Here and there, fresh ground had been dug up. I stood in Pa's shadow as we stopped at each cross, the weathered ones and the new pine ones. No Jacobs. Then we looked over at three fresh graves. All were unmarked.

"Doubt anyone would give him a marker. Nobody here would even know him long," Pa said.

"If Grandpa's gone, we never mourned him proper and said prayers over him. We never said goodbye like most folks do with their family."

Where are you, Grandpa?

"Let's see first if Grandpa's livin' or dead. Or if there's anythin' we can do for him. Then it will be time to say prayers. We'll go into the village to ask about him."

We stepped out of the cemetery together. A breeze lifted up, summery light.

Go on ahead, Solomon.

On the path, everyone was hurrying to the Emancipation Day parade. The day was ahead of us. One old man limped up the path toward us. With each step he leaned to one side on a cane, then set his other foot down again and kept coming. Pa brushed past me like wind and my heart began to pound. Sometimes the body knows things before the head does. At least mine did at that moment. For my feet took off running ahead in the breeze Pa stirred up.

The old man had more wrinkles on his face that I ever thought possible, and every one of them wiggled when he saw me. All those marks lined up until they made the biggest curve. The smile pulled me right into that man's arms that were spread wide open to let me back in.

"Solomon! Isam!" Grandpa was shouting and crying at the same time. "You're together and safe!"

He pulled us round and round in a circle and never stopped talking. Pa and I were speechless. My eyes were all wet and I kept wiping them to see him close. Up and down, I studied all the details of Grandpa. The wide feet. Long fingers. Whitened hair and beard. That easy way of grinning he had, like sunshine peeping up in the morning and spreading light everywhere inside me. It was all the same, exactly as I'd remembered.

Finally Pa asked, "Wh . . . where have you been?"

"Crossed over on the ferry this very morning. Captain told all us coloured folk to go to Little Africa to see the parade. Though I said I had business at Bertie Hall, the others pulled me along. And you have found me *here!*"

"You healed up, Grandpa Jacob?"

"Church folks set my ankle. My hip's still hurtin' some. Old age I suppose. It's not broke but it's had enough of workin' hard."

"But, Grandpa, it's been over a *year* since we left you at that church."

"Didn't heal 'til Christmas. Church folks said it wasn't a good idea to come in winter. So I stayed on helpin' out with other runaways. Come spring, I caught influenza. Fever and cough for some months. Folks wouldn't hear of my leavin' 'til now."

Grandpa looked healthy. He still stood upright. And he was popping with questions about how the two of us came to both be standing there together in front of him. He kept squeezing our hands and shoulders to feel if we were real, and fingered the smooth Sunday clothes we wore. So bright he was, all lit up like he was the sun itself. We got busy right away telling him all about how we settled in Buxton and were reunited over the letter I sent. How I was learning in a proper school too and Pa and I had just got land right beside Levi's and we were planning on clearing it for a small farm.

With every word we said, Grandpa Jacob's eyes got bigger and bigger, shining out from under his shaggy eyebrows. "That's what I wanted for Solomon. Good schoolin' and a better life. Findin' a safe place where he can grow. It's all like a dream."

"I never figured you runnin'," Pa told Grandpa. "Why did you leave Georgia?"

Grandpa shrugged. "You ran. I never knew where. Both your ma and wife were sold off at auction. All I had left was Sol. And old Master had plans for him too."

Pa and I stared at one another.

"Solomon listened good to everythin'. That's what made the trouble. Say one thing to that boy and he'd do it before you could swallow. Anybody would want to buy a boy like him. Master planned to sell him."

I looked up at my grandpa, but not high up. We were almost the same height now.

"You never told me that, Grandpa."

"Lots I couldn't tell you. Didn't want you to worry, lookin' behind you all the time. Those slavecatchers were trackin' more than Levi. They were after you too."

"I was so worried when you stayed behind in Buffalo, Grandpa."

"If you'd stayed with me, you might never have reached freedom. If I died, you might have been lost forever on the other side. I couldn't risk that."

"I waited and waited for you," I said. "All the time we crossed the country, I wanted to drag Levi back. When Pa returned to me, it was the right time to search Little Africa for you."

"If you hadn't come back for me now, Sol," said Grandpa. "I'd never have found you. I would have roamed this country and maybe never saw my family again."

Pa set his arm on my shoulder. "My son sees the future — way ahead. That's what the young do. They show us things we could never imagine. Like how a slave boy can now read and write. "

"Grandpa's the one who always saw far ahead," I said. "I just went where he wanted me to go."

Grandpa shook his head. "It's your time now, Solomon. Got a whole free life ahead of you. Your pa and I will work hard to get that farm in place for you. Can't wait to see it!"

I didn't tell what I knew — that all the while, this whole year through, Grandpa had been calling me back home to him. *Wait on me, Solomon*, I heard him say. *Keep walkin'*, I had plainly heard his voice tell me that very morning. All I did was listen good, like he always taught me. That's how I found him at last. That's why I never dug my roots deep enough yet; I'd been waiting on him.

Then laughter rippled like strong arms all around us. John Bright was marching by with his drums booming. He looked over at the three of us.

"Solomon! Caught up with one another, I see! Welcome to freedom!"

We joined the long line of people laughing and singing and shouting down the trails through Little Africa. Not one axe swung. Everyone wore their best clothes. Some were crying beneath their smiles, like Pa and me. Now I understood that those kind of tears are just the shadow joy jumps out of.

Afterwards, tables were set out in the clearings underneath the trees, with picnic baskets full of roasted deer and turkey, raspberries and bread. We sat down and at once were surrounded by those I knew. Even Missus Forsyth came to sit down beside us like an old friend. Grandpa took her gloved hand in his and kept thanking her over and over again for taking care of Levi and me. She just glowed when she looked at the three of us, together at last.

Then Charley the storekeeper looked down at Grandpa's shoes, with their thin, cracked leather.

"After Sol and Levi left here, we kept hoping you would show up in Little Africa, so we kept an eye out. Now you've come, I believe this boy has something for you."

I suddenly remembered. I had carried them in my backpack across Canada and back. Quickly I scrambled to unload them.

Grandpa studied the shiny black boots. He picked one up and looked at it closely, even the soles and the stitching, and the extra shoelaces I had set inside. He was grinning ear to ear and soon we helped him kick off his old shoes and settle into the new boots.

"Now I can walk clear across Canada!" he shouted. "Sure feels steady on my old legs."

"You won't have to," said John Bright. "We'll get you back by train. If we all give our spare coins, you can buy tickets to Chatham."

John soon sent me around with a bucket. Workers flung

their spare pennies and coins into it. As I walked, I read aloud little snippets from Josiah Henson's autobiography to everyone. Everyone here knew of him and some older ones had even heard him preach in Little Africa years ago. Though some had heard of his book, most had not read it. They kept shaking their heads at such a thing a runaway slave had done. They were amazed that he had kissed Fort Erie ground and learned to read from his own son. All begged to hear the part about Josiah's arrival, to compare to their own:

"I was a stranger, in a strange land, and had to look about me at once, for refuge and resource. . . . I knew nothing about the country, or the people, but kept my eyes and ears open."

When I came around, someone raised their hand to hush the talking and everyone listened to the reading with wide eyes. The bucket soon grew heavy in my hands. We had all been strangers here once, but not anymore. At dusk, talk grew quieter. The men spoke about their futures.

"If slavery ever ends like the abolitionists say it will," Abram told us, "and all's safe, I'd go back home."

Henry agreed. "Me too. Look for my family and start up a new life."

Pa said best what was in my heart. "Not me. This country rescued me. Here I got family, friends and my own land. I got a home right here."

"We three are going up to Buxton," I told them. "We won't ever leave there!"

"The son of my son is free!" Grandpa announced. "My own grandson readin' to all how a slave escaped to Canada. Imagine one of us tellin' their story to the world and all the folks

223

here listenin'. My long-gone son returned and plannin' to settle on a farm. I have lived to see all this. Worth every mile we took."

By a bonfire, musicians began playing songs we knew from back home. John Bright's drums banged, a banjo plucked and someone's voice lifted in the air.

The tallest tree in Paradise,
the Christians call the tree of life;
and I hope that trumpet might blow me home.

Blow your trumpet, Gabriel,
Blow louder, louder!
And I hope that trumpet might blow me home.

John Bright's grandchildren tumbled out into the middle of the clearing. The littlest ones lifted high on their tiptoes and twirled. Their brothers and sisters and cousins hollered and danced. Pa started stomping and Grandpa banged his cane down and hopped on his left foot then skipped on his right foot. Each time he lifted a boot up in the air, he shook it and laughed. So I leaped right in and bounced up and down, my feet springing light as rabbit claws on the flat earth. I was aiming to jump high as the moon and land back down to touch free ground. Whooping shouts flew out of me, echoing all through the trees.

Grandpa knew where I wanted to sleep that warm night. We spread straw outside and piled it high and flopped down. The stars pressed close down on top of us like a blanket. Seemed we were held like a sandwich between the sky above and the free ground beneath our backs.

I let out a big sigh.

Pa was on my right side. Grandpa Jacob was on my left. The stars were above us. And this whole free country spread out forever far beneath our feet.

We'd finally crossed over to the other side.

ACKNOWLEDGEMENTS

This novel could not have been written without the aid of many individuals and institutions, whose participation provided the groundwork for the research process:

Sandy Bogart Johnston, my tireless editor, and also Diane Kerner, Director of Publishing at Scholastic Canada, for their belief in this book when it was just an image of a school that kept Blacks out in the cold; Dr. Karolyn Smardz Frost, archaeologist, historian and author, for her detailed manuscript consultation and suggestions; Bryan Prince, historian, author, Board Member of the Buxton National Historic Site & Museum, for his wealth of knowledge, generosity of spirit and wonderful laugh that is now John Bright's laugh; Shannon Prince, Curator of the Buxton National Historic Site & Museum and her entire staff, with special thanks to Spencer Alexander for his cemetery tour; Barbara Hehner for her fact finding; Karin Foster, Archivist, Grey Roots Museum, Owen Sound, for her supporting materials; Gwen Robinson, leader of the Chatham-King Black Historical Society, WISH Centre, Chatham, for opening the doors to her centre and sharing her time; Jude Scott, Assistant Curator, Fort Erie Historical Museum, for providing research materials; June Spear, Administrator, Bertie Hall, Fort Erie, for her generous loan of materials; Fort Erie Public Library; Wilma Morrison, Administrator of the Norval Johnson Heritage Centre, Niagara Falls; Robert Neil, Chatham; Charles Davies, author, Fort Erie, for local history; Sinclair Tyios for Ontario research; and Neil Schwartz for his constant support, technical expertise and love of history.

226

AUTHOR'S NOTE

How does a story begin? With questions. Puzzles that keep you awake at night. Wonderings. What you don't know and must know. What haunts you.

My readers first dropped those questions like little seeds after my first two books on slavery were published: *If I Just Had Two Wings* and *Send One Angel Down*. On book tours, school visits, and in letters, my readers were all curious about the "afterlife" of ex-slaves who entered Canada in the nineteenth century: *What was freedom like for them? Did Canadians accept them? How did they live? What happened to their families? Were they reunited? Did they ever think back about their lives in slavery? What was it like to begin a new life?* To these questions, I added my own: *What kind of person made it to Canada, the terminus of the Underground Railroad? When did the ex-slaves really "cross over" to truly feeling free?*

I did not have the answers. So I took a journey on one of the paths runaway slaves took — on the Underground Railroad from Buffalo into what is now southwestern Ontario — to investigate their settlements, interview their descendants and do research. Luckily, a companion showed up, and that I will tell you about later. But first, let's look at the movement of ex-slaves from the South and free Blacks from the northern U.S. who fled across the United States/Canadian borders in the period before the Civil War.

Several major legislations were catalysts for this movement. In Upper Canada, Lieutenant Governor John Graves Simcoe, a known abolitionist, passed an Act of 1793 that supported the eventual end of slavery in Canada, stopped the importation of new slaves and ensured the freedom of slave children. In 1819, Canada West refused U.S. requests to return runaways. By 1834, Britain's Emancipation Act had abolished slavery in Canada and the British Empire. However, in the U.S. the second Fugitive Slave Act of 1850 facilitated the return of all runaways anywhere in the United States, even in previously "safe" northern states. Formerly enslaved and already free African Americans flooded the borders into Canada, about 35,000 in all, prior to the U.S. Civil War. There were few other places to go.

Soon after the end of the War of 1812, settlements had expanded in what is now southwestern Ontario, near ports of entry or areas with access to large tracts of land: Wilberforce, near London; Owen Sound in Grey County; Collingwood on Georgian Bay; the Queen's Bush; Dawn, near Dresden; Sandwich Industrial Mission, near what is now Windsor; Buxton; the Refugee Home Society; and Puce. Individual towns and cities also attracted the new arrivals: Windsor, Amherstburg, Colchester, Chatham, Dresden, London, Owen Sound, Hamilton, St. Catharines and Toronto.

As a teacher, I was particularly interested in knowing about the education offered at the time these people entered Canada, as this would be the turning point for their children's future. The general state of education in Canada West before 1840 was dismal, sparse, unequal, differing from area to area, and included mainly the privileged. Only half of all children in the country attended school. Into this situation, the new African Canadians emigrated.

There were many incidents of exclusion and discontent as white settlers reacted to the rapid influx of these newcomers into their communities. In some areas they encountered resistance, while other places were more welcoming, particularly large cities like Toronto. But everywhere, from Chatham to Sandwich and other small towns, there were rumblings of discord and prejudice against the African Canadians. Initially, poorly funded mission schools associated with churches educated these students, though many children did not attend school at all. When Dr. Egerton Ryerson, the Superintendent of Education in Canada West, drafted the Common School Act in 1850, his intention was to equalize educational opportunities by giving Roman Catholics permission to open their own schools where wanted. However, local white areas across Canada West used this law as an opportunity to exclude Black children from their schools, since Blacks could have their own schools too, though many never formed. It is in this milieu that my story takes place.

Newly arrived children who had lived under slavery entered school at a great disadvantage. Most, particularly from the deep South, likely had little prior schooling, and were often separated from family. Poorly trained teachers were overwhelmed by the needs of the new arrivals. My character, Solomon, met with the problems a new immigrant in any country faces; his own language and culture had to be replaced by another. He needed time to absorb and learn. For such a task, he needed mentoring from a teacher such as Mister Dillon.

Many true events are included in this novel and inspired its writing. One of the first things I saw upon entering Canada through Buffalo into Fort Erie was a plaque dedicated to those escaped slaves who crossed by ferry there. I immediately felt exhilarated that this would be the spot where my characters would cross over. Another true event was the yearly Emanation Day Parades marking the end of slavery in the British mpire, as declared by Queen Victoria on August 1, 1834. (Note that the U.S. Emancipation Day refers to U.S. President Abraham Lincoln's act of declaration setting slaves in rebel states free as of January 1, 1863; in the U.S. this event is celebrated on April 16.) Other real events include the drowning of Rodney Forsyth at fourteen; the "Select School" incident in Sandwich; the Willis family incident; Mary Ann Shadd's rescue of a boy from slavecatchers, and also the Alexander incident, both in Chatham; the murder of a Black boy in Chatham in 1812; the presence of The True Band in Chatham; the night school for adults at Reverend King's residence in Buxton; and Buxton's Liberty Bell.

* * *

Many historic people are characters in this novel. However, their dialogue and presentation are my own interpretation: Rodney Forsyth, Sarah Forsyth, John Bright, the Kival brothers, Mary Ann Shadd, Reverend William King, Mr. Sims of Buxton (who really did cross over at the suspension bridge), Father Thomas Henry Miller and Josiah Henson — who, though he never actually appears in the book, spreads his spirit over it. Although Old Ezekiel in this novel is fictional, he was based on the idea of the Griot, an important figure in African culture to the present day. The Griot is a preserver of ancient stories and traditions who kept history alive for his people over many centuries through oral storytelling and passing stories down to family members to preserve them. The Griot represents the power of words, of telling. This is the power that flows into Solomon. The fictional character of Mister Dillon was based on Master James Rapier, who taught at Buxton's SS#13 in 1861. A graduate of Buxton's school himself, Rapier eventually became active in Southern U.S. politics.

Actual "crossing over" sites used as a setting for this novel are: Michigan Street Baptist Church, Buffalo; Bertie Hall and tunnel, Fort Erie; Little Africa, Fort Erie (although little remains of this once flourishing community today other than the cemetery); Miller's Shipyard, Port Stanley; Port Burwell; the Detroit River and the Niagara River. Even Lake Erie, when fully frozen over in the deep winter, could be walked across. Bloomfield School and its lean-to for non-whites, the Princess Street School for Blacks in Chatham, and the Buxton settlement and its Mission School, all existed. Although the Buxton Mission School was very successful, it is no longer in existence, so Buxton school life in this novel was based on my research visits to North Buxton's SS#13, opened in 1861. You can see photos of this restored schoolhouse on the website of the Buxton Museum.

Finally, I wrote this novel because one afternoon, a boy with a bright face, almond eyes and big ears appeared in my imagination. As soon as I saw him, I knew why he had come. He was the companion who would guide me on the journey back to 1857, the one I'd been waiting for.

"All you have to do is give a long listen," he told me. "Hear what I have to say — truth waitin' to be told. And you must promise to tell them everything."

I did listen and, bit by bit, wrote down all I heard. The boy stayed with me for two years as I researched and wrote this story. His name was Solomon. He did answer many of those questions that had once haunted me. So I kept my promise to him and told you everything too.

Virginia Frances Schwartz

Quotation on page viii from "O Brothers, Don't Get Weary," *Slave Songs of the U.S.* by Allen, Ware & Garrison, New York, A. Simpson & Company, 1867.